SKYE

Also by Lauran Paine
in Thorndike Large Print

THE MARSHAL
TANNER

SKYE

Lauran Paine

Thorndike Press • Thorndike, Maine

Library of Congress Cataloging in Publication Data:

Paine, Lauran.
  Skye.

  1.Large type books. I. Title.
[PS3566.A34S55 1986]   813'.54   86-5784
ISBN 0-89621-718-3 (lg. print : alk. paper)

Large Print edition available through arrangement with
Walker and Company, New York.

Cover design by Abby Trudeau.

Cover illustration by Deborah Pompano.

CONTENTS

CHAPTER 1

A Town Called Powell

Frank Cutler had spent eleven years on the southern desert and excluding an occasional Saturday night in some town with a name like Terlingua or Cayonosa had taken no time off, and this was the year he was not going to work for anyone. So he lashed his bedroll above the saddlebags and behind his cantle, got a new set of plates all around on his *grulla* horse, and told the Terlingua blacksmith he was going to head north and keep riding until when he said *"buenas dias,"* folks would wonder what he was talking about.

It seemed destined to be a good year for saddle-tramping, except for the wind in Texas for which Frank had never been able to find any reason at all, except that each early springtime it came to roil clouds of dust, crack the soil, make folks irritable, and put grit in a man's meals.

He rode north, made mostly dry camps but occasionally found water to camp by, and eventually turned westward in the direction of New Mexico. He rode for forty days, through all of March and part of April, and had an idea that he was out of Texas but was unsure until he was driven by a torrential downpour into an adobe and slab-board town with the name of Powell. For that matter he was not sure that March had ended, but he thought it had; and when he got his horse taken care of at the livery barn and went up to the Powell rooming house to settle in until the storm passed, the fading, buxom, hard-eyed landlady said it was the second week of April. She told him he had been in New Mexico since crossing the north-south stage road back where he had noticed a cairn of whitewashed rocks meant to mark the point of separation. Then she had stood in the doorway watching Frank slap his saddlebags across the back of a chair and unroll his blankets atop the iron cot, and had said, "If you're running, you're safe enough providing there's no posse with a federal lawman in it. Federal lawmen can cross lines where state and territorial lawmen got no business trying."

Frank finished and straightened up. The

landlady was still there. He smiled and said he was not running, he was loafing, and the hard-eyed woman came as close to smiling back as she had probably come to smiling back at any man in years. She hauled upright off the door-frame, smoothed her dress, and said, "The food at the Powell café'll take the lining off your stomach, unless you been eating Mex food so long you don't have any lining. . . . I got some fresh coffee and roast beef with spuds in the kitchen. I don't run a boardinghouse, but you look like a drowned rat and you proba-bly haven't eaten a decent meal in a long time." She paused, still making her appraisal. "The stove'll dry out your clothes and all. I got some malt whiskey to lace the java with, and that ought to warm you up."

Frank's quiet gaze lingered on the woman. He was an individual with excellent percep-tion. At forty-four and even having spent most but not all of his years in the *despoblado* country of Texas — "the unpopulated place" — he was a fair judge of humanity, its motiva-tions, and designs.

On the other hand, laced coffee along with roast beef and potatoes near a hot stove under a roof that did not leak was an almighty temp-tation. And the buxom woman was not wear-ing a wedding band. He went with her down a dingy corridor which had closed, numbered doors on each side, with no idea whether the floor squeaked beneath his solid heft because of the drumroll of heavy rainfall overhead, and they entered a large kitchen filled with an aroma that attacked his senses in a way lavender hair scent and lilac body powder never had.

Her name was Mary and she had been married. In fact she and her husband had bought this rooming house so that when he retired they could still survive.

"He got killed," she said in a flat voice while putting a heaping platter of food on the oil-cloth-covered table in front of Frank Cutler. "No goddamned reason for it, Mister Cutler. . . . He was the constable here in Powell. No goddamned reason for it at all. One afternoon some freighters rendezvoused east of town, six wagons and fourteen men. They came into town, had some trouble at the general store, then went down to the saloon and had more trouble, and when my husband walked in they shot him. He hadn't even cleared the doorway. Hadn't said a word to any of them. Drunken scum."

Frank ate, drank coffee, and had no intention of opening his mouth in the face of her fierce bitterness.

"And do you know what this town did, Mister Cutler? Sam had been their constable for seven years. Kept the peace, helped drunks home, minded things, kept folks safe. . . . They did not do a damned thing. The freighters hitched up and headed north, and there wasn't a soul in this town that would make up a posse and go after them. You know what the town councilmen told me? No one was empowered by the law to go after those men and fetch back the ones who had killed my husband. They said Sam had been the only duly authorized lawman and he was dead, so they'd give him a good burial and all, but that was all they could do."

She poured another cup of coffee, added whiskey, and sat opposite him, her knuckles white around the cup, her pale blue eyes like wet talus. "You know what I told them, Mister Cutler?"

Frank pushed aside the empty platter and reached for his cup. "No, ma'am."

"Told them . . . I said to them all, sitting in their chambers behind the general store . . . I said you yellow-bellied sons of bitches, the reason you won't go after those men is because you're scairt peeless of them. . . . And I'm going to stay in this town so's every one of you will have to look me in the face as long as

11

you live, an' when your children come around, I'm going to tell them about the day Constable Sam Kilgallen was murdered in the saloon doorway, and what was done about it."

Frank sipped laced coffee and looked slightly to the right of her shoulder, and waited. The canker was old and deep, and it had left her face lined with its poison. But the whiskey and coffee were bringing color to her cheeks, and there was nothing left for her to say, so, by inches, the fury diminished until she eventually arose to get the pot and refill both their cups.

Later, when Frank went out front to the roofed-over porch to breathe the wet night air and study the lights across the road, he let out a long gush of pent-up air. For forty days he had encountered only an occasional rattler or lizard, little desert swift fox, or foraging coyotes. He had spoken to his *grulla* horse, and for a time he had forgotten about people. Now, he was back among them again, and tomorrow morning he would roll out on the wrong side of human nature again.

There was not a single rig or saddle animal tied at the racks on either side of the chocolate-colored millrace that was Powell's wide main thoroughfare, and except for the livery, the poolroom, and the saloon there were no lights burning.

But the downpour seemed to be lessening; at least the sounds were softer although the rain was still coming down straight.

He made it across through ankle-deep mud to the saloon, scraped his boots off, and entered. There were three men at the bar, four old gaffers at a table near the big iron cannon heater stove playing toothpick-poker, and an unsmiling, portly man polishing glasses behind the bar. The only man who noted Frank Cutler's entrance was the round-faced barman. He nodded and as Frank leaned on the bar the barman set up a bottle and a glass, then shook his head as he said, "Sometimes I wonder why anyone stays in this damned country. We get eight months of drought when it's so hot it'd melt the *cojones* off a brass donkey, then we get a week of rain like a fat cow peein' on a flat rock."

Frank was sympathetic as he poured. "It's pretty much the same any place a man goes." He lifted the jolt glass and smiled, but the barman was unappeased as he turned to go wait on the three range men farther along the bar.

A young cowboy entered and halted to shake like a dog before advancing on the bar. He had taffy-colored hair, slate-gray eyes, needed shearing almost as badly as Frank, and wore an old Colt with a pair of yellowing ivory grips. His shirt and britches were faded to a uniform pale blue, his boots were run-over and scuffed, and when he leaned to address the barman Frank thought he looked thirty and was perhaps eighteen, because everyone who lived out of doors always got a grainy look to them.

It was pleasant in the saloon. The stove kept things warm, there were not enough customers for the place to be noisy, and so, though drying attire added to the oniony scent of old sweat and tobacco smoke, Frank relaxed in comfort. He was perfectly at home in an atmosphere someone had once likened to a boar's nest.

Too, the whiskey was mellow. He rolled and lit a smoke. When the barman drifted down and said, "That range man says it's letting up outside," Frank nodded and smiled. He wanted to move on, and perhaps if the ground wasn't pure gumbo come morning he would be able to.

Four newcomers shouldered in out of the night, large, noisy men with checkered flannel shirts under stained, old horsehide coats. Their hats were shapeless and water-darkened. They wore the heavy, flat-heeled boots of freighters, and when the barman looked at them, Frank watched his color fade and his eyes widen.

The old men playing sham poker also looked at the newcomers, then stopped dealing cards, and sat like shriveled carvings as the big men stamped off mud on their way to the bar and a black-headed freighter with tight, curly hair and a trimmed beard to match rattled backbar bottles with a big fist brought down hard on the counter.

The barman brought two bottles and four glasses, and did not once raise his eyes as he set them up and shuffled toward the upper end of his bar to lean and make several wide swipes across the wood with his rag.

Two of the men who had been at the bar when Frank arrived put down coins and left. The old gaffers also departed, pausing at the door to button their coats to the gullet and yank down their hats.

Frank dropped his smoke and stepped on it; then he raised his head as a barrel-sized freighter shouldered the young cowboy to get more room and turned with a smile and a challenging look. Frank had first seen that expression when he had been thirteen. Since then he had seen it many times. He had taken exception to it at thirteen and ever since then.

The bar was twenty feet long with only

seven men ranged along it. No one had to push anyone. There was room enough.

The taffy-haired range man yielded, but the knuckles on his jolt glass were white.

The freighters were loud, bullying men, who slugged whiskey straight down as though it were water. Frank saw the barman's expression and thought of what the rooming house landlady had told him no more than an hour earlier.

The barrel-shaped man shouldered the cowboy again, making a sly game of it and grinning. Frank sighed; the freighter was a fool. If he hadn't been, he would have recognized the signs: the younger man gazing steadily from an expressionless face at his whiskey glass.

The freighter loosened his long horsehide coat to scratch, and the old long-barreled Colt in its holster was exposed. He spread both arms atop the bar, nudging the cowboy, and Frank saw it coming before anyone else did. The taffy-haired younger man twisted from the waist, reached with his left hand, grabbed a fistful of flannel cloth, swung the older and heavier man half around, and dropped him like a stone with a fisted set of bony knuckles squarely between the eyes.

The loudness became a shocked pause

which stretched into a long silence as every-one in the saloon stopped talking, and, except for the remaining three freighters, stopped moving. They stepped back a little to gaze from the unconscious man to the young range rider.

The curly-bearded freighter with black eyes and a wide, thin mouth was the last of them to raise his eyes to the cowboy.

The barman remained up at the north end of his bar, where he called out, "That's enough. You there, cowboy, you get out of here." There was no authority in his voice, and no indignation either.

The freighters did not even turn to look up there. The large black-eyed one methodically eased back his coat without taking his eyes off the cowboy. His companions shuffled slightly to one side, also getting ready.

Frank was southward, directly behind the cowboy, a very poor place to be. The cowboy did not move; he faced three men who had been drinking, all of them older and more ex-perienced than he was. Frank would have cursed with disgust another time, but not now, not when he was going to be hit when the fight started.

Nor did he like what was shaping up; the range man was a fool, but the freighters were worse — they were bullies who were going to kill a man they outnumbered and could probably outshoot as well.

All that was really required under these circumstances was for the freighters to keep the range rider there until they could rouse the barrel-shaped man, then turn him loose to teach the cowboy a lesson.

CHAPTER 2

Making Tracks

The large black-eyed man stood completely still and silent for so long Frank was beginning to wonder whether he would ever move. Then he said, "You goddamned bastard."

The cowboy did not seem to be breathing. No more than fifteen feet separated them. No one walked away from this kind of a fight.

Frank very slowly edged to his left away from the cowboy, behind him but also a yard or so to his left side. The freighters flicked glances, but very briefly. They were concentrating on the cowboy. Frank took down a shallow breath and let it out slowly. Then he said, "Go ahead, gents," and waited.

This time when the freighters looked at him, their eyes lingered. They were momentarily surprised, probably because they had been sure the cowboy was alone. They had to

19

adjust to an altered situation, which Frank understood and took advantage of. "Well . . . you going to wait for morning?"

The black-eyed freighter's expression did not change, but his companions were made differently. Their eyes darted from *two* adversaries at fifteen feet to the large man with the curly cropped beard.

The black-eyed man moved, and before his gun was high enough to tip, Frank shot him through the middle of the brisket. The other two freighters were even slower. Frank shot the man almost directly facing him, and the taffy-haired cowboy fired simultaneously at the third freighter. The cowboy's bullet was a foot wide, the freighter's bullet splintered the bar front, and they both were desperately hauling back to fire again when Frank yelled "Hold it!" He had his barrel pointed directly at the freighter, the hammer back, his finger curled inside the trigger guard. A sensible man would have obeyed, or perhaps the freighter wanted to stop and couldn't, but whatever the reason, he fired; the cowboy fired even as he was striking the splintered bar front, and Frank squeezed off his third shot.

There was greasy smoke in the air which did not rise very rapidly, and there was not a spectator in sight for a long while, and then the portly barman's head appeared very slowly above the counter.

Frank looked at the motionless sprawl of arms, legs, and heads; he looked over where the cowboy was trying not to bend over, saw the ripple of jaw muscle, and moved forward to grab a chair and push it under the cowboy. He put up his six-gun and forced the doubling-over younger man to sit back. There was torn cloth and blood. The bullet had gouged meat and muscle between the cowboy's side and his left arm, on the inside. The wound was painful, but the shock of being hit by a bullet was worse. Frank pried the ivory-handled Colt loose, dropped it into the cowboy's holster, picked up his hat, shoved it on his head and said, "Get up."

The barman and his only remaining customer were up at the north end of the bar, white as ghosts, looking at the devastation, the blood and death.

Frank yanked the cowboy to his feet and pushed him toward the door. Outside, a chilly, soggy little gusty wind was blowing. Frank said, "Where is your horse?"

For the first time, the cowboy spoke. "At the livery barn."

Frank pushed him roughly again. "So is

mine. Walk and keep walking."

"I'm hit."

"You'll be hit a lot worse if you don't get on your horse. There's a town constable somewhere around here, and maybe more freighters. Keep walking."

They made it to the livery barn where a horrified nightman stood gaping as they saddled their horses. He finally said, "Jesus, mister, someone better do something. Your friend's bleedin' like a stuck hawg."

Frank flipped the nightman a silver cartwheel, waited for the cowboy to mount, then swung up and led the way through the mud up the dark back alley to the rooming house.

Ten minutes later they broke clear of Powell riding north through a dismal drizzle. Above them pale stars cast a diffuse and useless light through the wet. There was no moon, and occasionally a soggy, ground swell breeze alternately blew from the north and the northeast.

The younger man rode stoically, and Frank was not disposed to conversation either. He was never a talkative individual, and under the present circumstances he was even less so.

They were leaving tracks a small child could read, but there was nothing to be done about that except to ride long enough and far enough to outdistance pursuit. All in all,

Frank was not worrying; but by the time they found game trails which led easterly to the north-south stage road and left the timber for the roadbed, he was beginning to feel annoyed.

It had been his intention to head up this way in the morning, so perhaps he'd gained a little time by leaving when he did, but he never for a moment expected to ride out of Powell with a shot-up companion with whom he'd killed three men.

They halted once near the top-out of a pass neither of them had ever seen before, then with the sky clearing and a colder wind arriving, they settled for the long ride downhill. About an hour before dawn, with daylight close, Frank halted near a cold-water creek, made a small fire to warm his companion, and led their animals into a glade to graze hobbled. Then he returned and roughly examined the younger man.

The wound was trickling blood and there was purple swelling, but, barring infection and given sufficient time, it would heal and the taffy-haired man would recover. Frank made a shirttail bandage, untied the range man's jacket and got it around him, then stoked up the fire and rolled a smoke. "What's your name?" he asked him.

"Sam Morton. What's yours?"

"Frank Cutler . . . How old are you, Sam?"

"What difference does that make?"

"Some," stated Frank, getting comfortable by the fire and eyeing his companion. "If you're young, then maybe being a damned idiot is excusable. If you're not young, then you are a worse kind of a fool. There were three of them. At that distance you were fixing to commit suicide. Let me tell you something, at fifteen feet gunfights don't determine who is best, only who is left, and at those odds back yonder, it wasn't going to be you."

The slate-gray eyes were fixed on Frank Cutler. For a long time Sam Morton said nothing. He gingerly fingered his bandage, then he leaned down on his good side close to the flames and finally he spoke.

"What would you have done, cut and run?"

Frank thought, then shrugged. "Yes, if I could have."

"Well, I'm no goddamned coward, Mister Cutler."

Frank pitched his quirley into the fire. "No. You're a fool. . . . I don't expect anyone will be after us. Not close anyway. All the same we'd better keep moving."

"Mister Cutler?"

"I told you my name is Frank."

"Why did you buy in?"

"I was standing behind you. Bullets going through you were going to hit me. Get up. I'll fetch the horses."

"Frank."

"What."

"You beat everyone."

Frank could make out wonderment, and perhaps a little suspicion, in the younger man's face. "So you think I'm some kind of gunman. Sam, I spent a long time being alone in a lonely country, and I practiced mumblety-peg until I broke my knife blade then I practiced with my guns." He walked back for the horses and fifteen minutes later with sunshine coloring the topmost rims, they were nearing the lower country with open grassland for miles onward.

They made a camp along a creek after the sun was high and there was pleasant warmth. Sam had jerky and dried apples. Frank had coffee, whiskey, and three little fat tins of sardines in oil. Afterward they slept. Three hours later they struck out again. By nightfall the taffy-haired man's wound was swollen to several times what it had been, he was in considerable pain, and the discoloration worried Frank, but he did not allow his worry to show.

They camped early, while there was still daylight. Frank boiled water and washed the wound, rebandaged it, and boiled coffee. Sam Morton had a fever; he would neither eat nor drink any of Frank's coffee and did not meet the older man's gaze.

While the fire was still burning, Sam fell into a sweaty sleep, Frank went up the nearest slope and tried to get some idea of the land before visibility got too impaired.

There was either a large ranch northward and near some broken country, or a town. If it was a town it was small enough to be considered a village, and if it was a cow outfit, it was large enough to employ perhaps as many as ten range men.

He returned to their camp, considered the younger man's feverish, sweat-shiny face, wagged his head, and turned in. Whatever that was up ahead, a ranch or a village, they were going up there tomorrow. He was not very hopeful of finding a medical practitioner, they were uncommon even in moderately large towns, but there would be medicine and possibly someone more skilled than he was.

He had a private idea why Sam Morton looked so flushed, feverish, and sweaty. He had seen gangrene before. If that was what it was, then nothing anyone could do would keep the taffy-haired range man alive for very long.

Frank was roused while it was still dark. The rain clouds were shredded, there were diamond-chip stars showing, and although he had no sensation of having slept, he had. He lay still trying to imagine what had awakened him, and the answer came when one of their horses snorted and struggled to flee despite his hobbles.

Frank rolled out, palmed his handgun without bothering to get into his boots, went down where their mounts were standing so close they touched, both heads pointing northward. He sat down in some underbrush and waited. It was wolves, five or six of them, and they were more curious than hungry, but just their smell had the hobbled horses steeped in terror.

A large gray bitch with a sloping rear and a broad, flat head came into the clearing and walked deliberately in the direction of the horses. Frank shot her through the head, the explosion panicked the horses, the remaining wolves fled like gray rags flung at random against the darkness, and before the echoes got lost amid the surrounding timber, Frank went among the horses talking them down from their panic.

After a while and when daylight was brightening the eastern curve of the world, Frank returned for his boots, shirt, and hat to find Sam Morton sitting bolt upright in his blankets clutching a Winchester.

Frank put twigs on the coals, blew up a flame, then said, "Wolves. Scairt hell out of the horses." Then he regarded the taffy-haired man, who was holding the carbine in both hands. "You feeling better?"

Sam, having been awakened by gunfire, had a wildly beating heart and did not answer immediately, but eventually he said, "Yeah. Did you shoot them?"

"Shot one, the lead bitch." Frank arose with both boots on, shoved in his shirttail, dropped his hat on, and went closer to look. The swelling was less, and although the discoloration still looked terrible, clearly Sam Morton had improved during the night. Frank said, "I thought it was gangrene. I figured you was going to die on me."

Sam Morton looked up. "I was trying to, then someone shot a gun close by, and it scairt me so bad I had to see what was happening."

Frank laughed, then went in search of more twigs for the fire. When he returned the cowboy was down at the creek gingerly trickling cold water over his bandaged left arm, and left side. When Frank had the coffee boiling and the last of their food ready to eat, Sam walked back, worried his coat on, and leaned with his upper body toward the blessed heat.

Dawn was cold, as it always was at that elevation, but at least the heavens were clear which meant the rain would not return. For a while anyway.

They did not strike camp until about noon. They talked and soaked up heat, and never once mentioned those three dead men back at Powell. When they finally rigged out and rode away, Frank wagged his head. If he'd got that wound, he'd be sick as a dog; it was wonderful to be eighteen or nineteen. The dismaying part of it was that a man did not know how wonderful it was.

Sam drew his ivory-stocked six-gun and said, "It belonged to my pa." Then leathered the weapon and rode a short ways in silence before speaking again. "My ma died when I was born, back at Council Bluffs. My pa brought me west, and the cholera got him four years ago. Down near a place called Tanque Verde."

Frank waited for the rest of it, but Sam only said, "What about you?"

For some distance Frank rode in quiet thought. He was forty-four and everything he knew, or that had happened during all that time, could have been telescoped into a couple of sentences. "Nothing much. I came out from Missouri. I was an orphan. Don't know anything about my folks. The people I came west with bound me out to a sagebrush stockman and I stayed until I was about your age, then started hiring out. Been working livestock ever since."

Sam's gaze was skeptical. "You shoot good," he said.

Frank understood the inference. "Well, when you're alone most of the time, like I told you, you do something to break the monotony."

Sam did not believe him. Frank could feel it without looking at the younger man. Nevertheless, he had told the truth. Well, there had been a few interludes, but they hardly amounted to the kind of things that influenced a man toward whatever he ultimately became.

They rode in the direction of those buildings Frank had noticed earlier, but when they were atop a low land swell with fair visibility, it turned out not to be a town but a large cattle operation, so they turned north and continued to ride. Frank was not eager to hire on, and Sam was not in any shape to. Also, Frank wanted more distance between them and the town of Powell.

They were skirting the base of some timbered hills but remaining out in open country, when they saw several fish hawks soaring and circling. Frank turned up through the timber, sashayed for a decent game trail, and led the way for two miles to the grassy verge of a large lake.

Sam sat looking around. Eventually he said, "Can you improve on this?"

Frank couldn't. They made an early camp, scouted a little on foot, then rummaged through saddlebags for their balls of fishline, tied the hooks and without any difficulty at all, caught six large speckled trout.

Later, full as ticks and warmed by a deadwood fire, Sam asked a question, "Where were you heading when you rode into Powell?"

"Nowhere. This season I'm goin' to loaf. Make a few camps like this one, and not do a blessed thing I don't want to do. Why?"

"Just curious is all."

"What are your plans?"

Sam settled closer to the fire before answering. "I thought I might go north and hire on somewhere. But maybe I won't. A man can't do much with a wound, can he?"

31

Frank dragged his bedroll to the fire and sat down on it. "How old are you?" he asked.

"Nineteen."

Frank rolled a smoke and lit it off a firebrand. He'd pretty much guessed it. "In the morning wash that wound again and we'll make a new bandage for it. Good night."

CHAPTER 3

A Surprise

On the sixth day, with a vast plateau on both sides and a good camp near a cold-water spring, the same thing which had happened to Frank before, happened again. He awoke with cold rainwater striking his face.

They struck camp in the dismal predawn, got astraddle wet saddle seats, and aimed for some distant hills made dark by standing timber.

It was a long ride. They slouched along in yellow slickers with water trickling down their necks in back, with more water running from the front droop of their hats, and about the time they were close enough to be able to make out some of the details of those timbered hills, an early and dismal end to this day was closing in.

They had barely spoken all day. Sam's arm

and side had no swelling now, but the scabbed-over, healing flesh itched.

Frank drew rein finally, dug among the contents of his saddlebags, and brought forth a greasy cloth that contained the last of their cold fish. They divided it without dismounting, while studying the soggy-looking uplands on their left. When they finished Sam said, "What choice we got?"

Frank's answer was short. "None."

He led the way into the timber, and up through there huge trees prevented all the cold rainwater from reaching them, which was at least a minor improvement.

It got dark faster where they were now riding than it did back out on the open grassland of the plateau they had crossed, and eventually, when they encountered immense outcroppings of dark rock, although it was only about suppertime, it might just as well have been midnight.

Frank picked his way carefully. His *grulla* horse was not entirely cooperative, not because of the rain — he was inured to that sort of thing — but he did not like the treacherous footing.

A soughing high wind swept through disturbing raindrops up there. They cascaded earthward with an icy touch.

Frank rode doggedly with his head pulled low and his narrowed eyes watching ahead. All they would need right now would be for one of the horses to get a bad stone bruise or a pulled tendon. Eventually, he swung off and led his animal.

Sam suddenly called and pointed with a rigid arm. Frank looked, saw the mouth of a huge cave in the rough rock wall on his left, and did not move for a long time. Then he motioned for Sam to come forward and hold his horse while he took his Winchester and clawed through underbrush to explore. Caves in this kind of country were bear dens, and any downpour at all was preferable to seeking shelter in a cave that had bears in it.

Normally, bear caves had a distinctive smell. If this one had a smell, or an inhabitant, Frank could not detect either. He walked ten feet inside; the darkness was like the bottom of a well. He groped for a stone and rolled it deeper into the darkness. Nothing happened, and if it had hit a rear wall he could not hear it because of the increasing muffled roar of rainfall outside.

He went back and gestured with the Winchester for Sam to bring the horses on up. The roof of the cave was easily three feet taller than the crown of Frank's hat, and the width of their sanctuary was roughly thirty feet. They had no idea how deep the cave was, not even after they had unsaddled and had found a huge pack rat's nest which they plundered of dry twigs for a fire.

The fire helped considerably — even the horses were content not to move out of its perimeter of warmth; and when Frank went to work boiling coffee, which was all they had left except for Frank's untouched pony of whiskey, Sam removed his slicker and the coat beneath it, then sat cross-legged as he removed his soggy bandages and propped them on sticks to dry.

Coffee was not a meal, but when it had been laced a little it made a fair substitute, for a while anyway. Frank drank his and rubbed a scratchy jaw. He gazed over at Sam who looked dirty, thin in the face, and covered with pale reddish whisker stubble. Sam smiled and spoke above the storm's constant muted roar. "Someone took pity on us."

Frank was hunched toward the fire with a tin cup in his hand. "God looks after fools, Messicans, and cowboys; that's his profession."

Fortunately, there was no wind and the rising heat tended to go back rather than forward toward the wide-open mouth of their cave. There was also improved visibility, but it did not reach to the back of the cave; and when Frank felt warm inside as well as outside, he left his Winchester leaning upon his saddle and went exploring toward the limit of firelight, and beyond.

He was satisfied that if there had been some kind of varmint in the cave, by now it would have fled, which meant there would be a rear opening somewhere.

But there was no rear opening, and there was no varmint. He stepped on dried bones which shattered underfoot, and he lit a sulfur match when he stepped through something that was soft and made a muffled sound. It was ancient ash inside a stone fire ring.

Before the match flickered out Frank saw something that stopped his breathing for two or three seconds. A wizened, seated man with two blankets, one under him, the other around his shoulders, was sitting far back looking steadily at him. Then the match went out.

Frank turned back with hair along the back of his neck standing up. When he reached the fire he drained what remained of his laced coffee and said, "There's a dried up old dead In'ian back there with his back to the wall. Shriveled up like old rawhide."

Sam was rewrapping the dried bandages. He said, "We're in a burial cave, Frank. I've heard of them but never saw one. How many are back there?"

"I saw only one. He was too far back in the darkness to make out much. He was sitting there on an old blanket looking straight at me."

Frank rolled a smoke and watched Sam wrap himself with the bandages. The wounds were much better. In fact nearly all the discoloration was gone. Sam was better too. It was probably the best gift of youth that recovery from illness and injury was fast.

Sam got his coat on and arose with the ivory-stocked six-gun riding loosely on his right hip. "I got to see," he said, and walked away.

Frank watched the horses for a while. They were no doubt hungry, but for a while anyway they would be perfectly content to stand inside out of the downpour with steam rising from their backs.

He went forward until rain mist struck him in the face, but it was impossible to see anything beyond the opening except the nearest big old pines and firs and some nearby underbrush. The rain had begun to increase in intensity about the time they had located the cave, and it had not slackened off since then. Frank wondered where they were, how long the damned storm would last, and what they were going to do for food.

He turned and went back toward the fire. Sam was squatting, making a wavery shadow against the south wall. He was gesturing. Frank stopped in his tracks. The mummified old Indian was sitting in front of Sam clutching his shoulder blanket with hands like claws.

Black eyes like coals swept past Sam to Frank. Then Sam looked around. "He was alive, Frank, and colder'n hell, so I brought him to the fire."

Frank sank to the ground and poked several more twigs into the fire, making it flare up. He stared at the old man. "Does he understand English, Sam?"

"Naw. He don't even understand my hand talk."

Frank eyed the wizened old face. He had met his share of redskins, and although what he did not know about them would have filled a bushel basket, there was one thing he *did* know: even the ones who could speak English were not likely to do so unless they damned well wanted to. But this Indian was very old, and for a fact those old ones rarely ever learned English. Frank said, "I guess the storm drove him in here too."

Sam shook his head. "Naw," he said, and held up something in his right fist. "He had two of these sacks of grub back there and a gourd as big as my head with water in it." Sam lowered the articles. "He's been in here a while, Frank. . . . I'll tell you what I think. His friends and family put him in here and gave him enough food to last until he died. They do that. Put the old ones somewhere and leave 'em to die."

Frank knew this and said nothing. The Indian looked as old as dirt. Frank thought he probably would not weigh a hundred pounds with rocks in his pockets. His blanket was old and threadbare, and his clothing was the same. Frank poured some whiskey into the coffee pan and set it close to the fire. While Sam was trying to draw the old man out, Frank filled a tin cup with whiskey-laced coffee and held it out. Without any hesitation the old man took it in both hands and noisily drank till the cup was empty.

The effect was almost instantaneous. The old bronco began to gently rock forth and back, clutching his blanket. He stared with sunken black eyes that glittered in the shifting light. He watched the flames with great intensity, then, without any preliminary, began to sing in a keening, undulating tone. It was the kind of sound that made the nerves of any non-Indian who had never heard an Indian chant crawl.

Frank rolled and lit a smoke, eyed the old man, and when Sam looked around, said, "Now we got a drunk In'ian for company."

Sam, who felt responsible for the old man, shrugged defensively. "At least he doesn't have a drum."

Frank was thinking of something else. Where there was one Indian, there were others. And while there had been no serious Indian trouble in many years in most places, among range men it was common knowledge that an occasional rider would disappear and never be heard of again, and that almost invariably happened in Indian country.

He killed his smoke and gazed toward the cave opening. Until he did that he had not realized that the downpour had been diminishing for some time and there was a little low wind coming up from the south which was warmer than previous winds had been. He arose and walked out as far as the opening. There were stars. They were not everywhere, which meant the massive overcast was still up there, but at least there were a few to the north and west.

He returned to the fire, which Sam had fed until there were moderately high little flames again. Sam pointed. The old Indian was lying with his back to the fire wrapped in his blanket sound asleep.

Frank sank down. "Maybe we can ride on in the morning," he announced. "I think the storm is leaving."

Sam nodded his head in acceptance of this good fortune, then he pointed. "What do we do with him?"

"He was here when we found this place, he'll be here after we leave it."

"Frank, he's old as hell and alone."

For a moment Frank simply gazed at his companion. "That's not our fault, Sam. You know why they put him in here."

Sam said no more for a long time. Then he delved through a saddlebag and pulled out a plug of molasses-cured Kentucky twist, gnawed off a corner, pouched the cud inside his cheek, and replaced the plug. A hurrying band of foraging coyotes came almost to the cave opening before they picked up the human scent and scattered, yapping in astonishment and fright.

Sam spat into the fire. "If that'd been wolves and we hadn't been in here, they'd have dragged the old man around and strung out his guts for a mile."

Frank got his bedroll close to the fire and kicked out of his boots. He sat looking at his companion. "What do you want to do — take that old scarecrow with us? Sam, for all we know we're in the middle of some damned reservation. All we got to do is get caught by that old man's family, and we'll end up under two tons of rocks down in some canyon where no one'll ever find us. Besides that, what would we do with him? You can't just go riding all over hell with a shriveled up old In'ian who looks like a monkey behind your saddle."

The rain stopped so suddenly it made both men turn toward the cave opening. Stars shone everywhere they could see, and that southerly wind Frank had noticed earlier was brisking up into a steady blow. It had warmth in it, but it was wind, and of all the elements a man had to contend with, Frank Cutler liked wind the least.

He rolled into his blankets half-believing the wind would be gone by morning.

CHAPTER 4

The Strangers

Up to a point, Frank's good luck held; there was no wind when he rolled out to stir coals and make the fire come to life. The old Indian and his blanket were gone. So was Frank's pony bottle of whiskey. He peered bleakly into the depths of the cave but did not go back there.

Sam awakened hungry and also noticed that the old bronco was gone. He was pulling on his boots when he asked if Frank had seen the Indian. Frank shook his head. He was also hungry, but he had coffee heating and that would help.

Sam went out front, saw their horses picking browse with their hobbles in place, and guessed that Frank had been up and stirring long enough to care for the animals. He was turning to reenter the cave when he distinctly heard voices. He stood perfectly still trying to place those sounds. The front of the cave had large trees in three directions, in the fourth, or easterly direction, there was a scrabrous, black bluff of which the cave was part. The voices seemed to be coming from the north, but until whoever was out there got much closer it would not be possible to see them.

Sam returned to the fire and told Frank what he had heard, then took a cup of hot coffee while Frank went out front.

There were three of them, range men from appearance, and they were working their way toward the cave through a countryside still dripping water although the sky was now cloudless and the sun was up.

Frank waited, trying to make out what the riders were saying, but when he got a good sighting he went back inside the cave and picked up his Winchester. Sam looked up at Frank's face, then arose without a sound and also picked up his saddle gun.

The range men came around through the big trees, saw two shaggy-headed, soiled, and silent men standing with Winchesters at the cave's entrance, and stopped in their tracks, clearly surprised.

One man was graying over the ears and appeared to be about Frank Cutler's age. He had a ruddy complexion, a drooping longhorn moustache, and flinty eyes beneath the droop of his hat. The other two were younger. Both were lean men with lined faces and perpetually squinted eyes. One was shorter than the other. The taller one was chewing a cud as all three of them sat gazing at Frank and Sam.

The older man finally spoke. "Morning, gents."

Frank nodded. "Good morning."

The graying man shifted slightly in his saddle, acting a little at a loss. Then he said, "You boys passing through?"

Frank nodded again but did not speak this time.

"Well," stated the graying man. "My name is Rand Belton. Range boss for Skye Cameron northwest of here a ways. . . . We're lookin' for an In'ian."

Sam said, "Up in here?"

Rand Belton smiled a little. "Yes. Before the rain we tracked him in this direction, up through here a ways, then it got dark and we went home."

"What kind of In'ian?" asked Sam.

"Arapahoe. This used to be their hunting ground."

Sam was silent a moment before asking another question. "Why are you lookin' for him, Mister Belton?"

It showed in the range boss's face that he did not like that. He eyed Sam a long time before saying, "You're on Cameron range, friend. What we do is our business."

From the corner of his eye Frank saw Sam gently haul up to his full height. He had done that back in the saloon at Powell before the fight started. Frank spoke quickly. "Mind describing this In'ian, Mister Belton?"

The range boss minded. He was getting angry. "In'ian," he told Frank. "Just an In'ian . . . Is he in that cave?"

Frank smiled a little. "As far as I know there is no In'ian in here. Maybe there was, but I haven't seen any In'ian this morning."

Rand Belton swung to the ground. His companions also dismounted. When all three of them started up through the underbrush toward the cave entrance, Frank said, "What do you want him for, Mister Belton?" and the rawboned, dark-eyed man halted; there was color in his face. He looked steadily at Frank a long time, then said, "Are those your horses down yonder in the grass?"

Frank nodded.

"Then you better get saddled up and on your way. On Cameron range we don't take kindly to trespassers."

Frank waited until they were emerging

from the undergrowth directly in front of the entrance, then he said, "Mister Belton, if you want to come inside you're going to have to tell us what you want the In'ian for." As he finished speaking Frank leaned his Winchester aside and straightened up less than forty feet from the foreman.

Rand Belton was at best a flinty man, a good stockman but not easy to work for, or with. He studied Frank for a moment before saying, "All right. For stealing cattle."

Sam Morton snorted. "Not by a damned sight. He didn't steal any cattle."

Belton pushed a few feet closer and halted again with his companion behind him, one on each side. "He's in there," Belton said to Sam, and was silent for as long as it took for him to reach a conclusion. "He didn't steal cattle by himself. There were others with him. . . . Where were you boys a week or so back?"

Sam reddened but before he could precipitate trouble Frank spoke up. "A long ways south of here coming through some hills and then across a big plateau. . . . How long ago did you lose cattle, Mister Belton?"

"Maybe a week, maybe ten days. We didn't discover it until we were moving heifers and bulls. A brockle-faced cow and the bunch she

48

grazed with were gone. Maybe twenty, thirty head."

"It was In'ians?"

"Yes. A line rider saw them. Three men a long ways off."

"How far off, Mister Belton?"

The range boss did not answer. He looked steadily at Frank, then started forward again — and this time he clearly was not going to stop.

Frank called softly. When the range boss looked up, Frank drew. Belton stopped. So did the riders behind him. It was not being under someone's gun that held them rooted, it was the speed of that draw. Frank said, "There was an old In'ian in the cave last night. This morning we haven't seen him. Mister Belton, he's as old as you and me together. He's been sitting in here a long time. He's as skinny as a snake and frail."

Belton looked above the gun. "He is an In'ian. We don't stand for them being on Cameron range. Old don't have anything to do with it."

Frank sighed and returned his weapon to its holster. Without taking his eyes off the Cameron riders he said, "Sam, go see if that old scarecrow went back where we found him, an' if he did, fetch him up here."

Sam leaned aside his saddle gun and disappeared toward the rear of the cave. After he had departed Rand Belton continued to eye Frank. When he spoke again, his tone was softer and different.

"Just passing through, eh? Mister, whoever you are, I got an idea it'd be better if you and your partner didn't hang and rattle too long. There's hundreds of miles of open country north of here. Two riders could get lost out there providing they got on their way and didn't stop."

Frank understood Belton's implication and ignored it. He knew Rand Belton because he had known at least two dozen men like him. "So you can hang the old redskin?"

Again Belton went silent and remained that way, even after Sam returned with the old Indian. Sunlight hurt the old man's eyes so he raised a hand to shield them as he considered the cowmen who were staring at him. One of Belton's riders spoke for the first time. "It couldn't have been him, Rand."

The range boss shot back a sharp retort. "Then whose tracks were those we followed almost up this far? It was the same sign those cattle thieves left. You saw that, Fred."

Fred protested. "Rand, that In'ian is too old. Look at him. He couldn't even set a horse, let alone — "

"Then there's another one in the cave," snapped the range boss, and Frank shook his head. "This is the only one in here, Mister Belton. . . . If there was another one, he was gone before Sam and I got up here during the storm last night."

Belton pursed his lips and expelled a hissing, long breath. He looked from Frank to the old man, his face stone-set in unrelenting lines. Then he wagged his head. "He knows. You can bet on that. The old bastard knows about those cattle."

Frank shrugged. "How are you going to make him tell you? He can't speak English. We tried it on him last night."

Belton had already evolved a plan. "He'll tell us, cowboy. We got a breed at the home-place who talks Arapahoe. He'll tell us, you can damned well bet on that."

Frank studied the three range men for a while then looked over at Sam as he said, "You win after all. We'll take him with us."

Belton's dark gaze jumped back to Frank Cutler. "You're not going to take him anywhere."

Frank put his head slightly to one side. "You expect to stop us, Mister Belton?"

"Not here, cowboy. You saddle up and try

51

riding very far. Cameron ranch's got six riders, not counting me. We'll stop you — dead."

Frank thought briefly, then said, "How far to your homeplace?"

"Maybe six, seven miles."

"We'll ride there with you, Mister Belton. All right?"

Rand Belton was far beyond any willingness to compromise. He also suspected a trick of some kind. But he had seen what would happen if he precipitated a fight, and that also contributed to his exasperation.

Very abruptly the old Indian sat down on the ground. He was unaccustomed to standing for very long. That caused a distraction and as the range boss glared at the old man, Frank said, "Sam, fetch the horses up here. We'll saddle up and go with these gents."

Sam hesitated because he did not like the idea of leaving Frank to face those odds. Then a more appealing thought occurred to him; he would be behind the Cameron riders, so he walked away.

There did not seem to be much point in trying to strike up a conversation with the range boss, so Frank leaned in the cave entrance, thumbs hooked, and said nothing. The old Indian pulled his threadbare blanket close and clutched it, although the ground was beginning to steam from hot sunlight. In broad daylight the old man looked even older and frailer, but his close-spaced black eyes were as bright and alert as the eyes of a lynx.

Rand Belton turned to look down past his men to where Sam had gone for the horses. Then as he turned back, he said, "What's your name, cowboy?"

"Frank Cutler. The other feller's name is Sam Morton."

Belton lifted his hat, scratched, and lowered the hat. "I'll tell you something, Cutler. There are In'ians in the mountains around here who are supposed to be on the reservation. Every cow outfit within five hundred miles has had trouble with them. Stealing, cutting fences, causing stampedes . . . My orders direct from Skye Cameron are not to take one damned thing off them. We've lost horses without a trace. They sneak off the reservation, steal, then sneak back."

Frank was interested. "Where is the reservation?"

Belton gestured. "North and east. They got enough land in it to take care of five times the In'ians they got on it, and the army has regular days for allotting beef. But they still sneak off and kill or steal cattle and run off horses. Folks are sick and tired of it."

53

"Tell the army, Mister Belton."

Belton's dark eyes flashed. He swore with heartfelt feeling, then he said, "You don't know anything about In'ians or the army, or you wouldn't say a thing like that. You can't tell the army *anything!*"

It was true that Frank Cutler knew very little about Indians, and less about the army, but over the years he had heard quite a bit about both, and right now he was willing to believe Belton's anger was probably justified. But Indian haters were not new to him either. He was fairly certain what would have happened to the old bronco if he had allowed the Cameron riders to take him away with them, and that did not sit well with him either.

Sam led the horses up. Frank did not turn his back on the Cameron riders. Sam led them into the cave, saddled both of them, and brought them back out. As he handed the reins to Frank, he said, "Who takes up the old man?"

Frank grinned. "You do."

Sam scowled. "So far today all I have been doing is taking orders."

Frank waited until Sam was mounted, then picked up the old man. He was surprised to find how light he was. As he settled him behind Sam's cantle he made a gesture for the

Indian to hold onto Sam's gun belt, then went after his own mount.

They followed the Cameron riders back down to the place they had left their mounts, and when the entire cavalcade was moving, Rand Belton rode up beside Frank and said, "You're running a hell of a risk over one old In'ian."

Frank gazed back. "What risk?"

Belton gestured with an outflung arm. "In twenty-four hours you could be so far off they'd never find you."

Frank studied the ruddy, lined, hard face at his side, then looked away without speaking, and Belton hastened ahead to take the lead.

CHAPTER 5

A Man Named Schmidt

Long before they reached the yard they encountered upgraded Texas razorbacks with quality bulls among them. To Frank it looked like Cameron — whoever he was — had a redback bull for about every forty or so cows, and he approved of that. He also approved of the upgrading program which had evidently been in progress for some time because every sassy fat calf he saw had a broader back and shorter legs than the cows they all came from.

Cameron ranch headquarters consisted of a sprawl of weathered log structures in a wide swale where there were trees and a white-water creek. It was an old place; aside from the buildings, which were numerous, generally large, and laid out in a very rough horseshoe shape around a yard of pure hardpan, there was the swale itself. It was at least fifty acres in size and had several fenced pastures not far from a network of working pole corrals.

Whoever Skye Cameron was, unless he was as old as the Indian clinging like a monkey to Sam Morton's gun belt, he had either bought or inherited this ranch, because it had clearly been established back in the days when a man took all he thought he might need, then twice as much again for good measure.

They dismounted at the rack out front of a massive log barn. Across the yard two men working in a three-sided blacksmith shop came to the front to look across the yard. One was wearing a shoeing apron and the other man had his right arm in a sling.

The silent riders with Rand Belton took all the horses inside to be cared for, and the foreman faced Frank and Sam with a wide-legged stance and bared his teeth in a bleak smile. He was on his own ground, among his own men. He said, "I'll tell you what I'm going to do, gents." He bobbed his head in the direction of the old Indian who was standing close to Sam Morton. "Lock that old son of a bitch in the smokehouse until it's decided what to do with him. . . . That's the cookhouse across the yard. It's close enough to dinnertime. The cook'll feed you. We'll grain your horses, then you ride out and don't come back."

Frank smiled back. "That's right decent of you, Mister Belton. I can see you are a neighborly person. But the In'ian eats with us. He hasn't had a decent meal for a longer time than we have. After that . . . I guess your boss will decide what happens."

Belton did not move nor change expression. "Do you think you got any chance at all if you try in this yard what you done at the cave? There's two fellers over yonder, there's me and the fellers who were with me this morning, and there's the cook." He turned slightly as the pair of lean men emerged from the barn after caring for the horses. Frank brought his head forward by saying, "Mister Belton, I got you figured for a smart man. I think you ought to let us feed the old man, then talk to your boss. Because I don't give a goddamn if you got fifty men around the yard, you'll be stone dead if trouble starts. A blind man couldn't miss you at this distance."

Sam Morton glanced at the pair of riders outside the front barn opening. They gazed back from expressionless faces. Those two over at the shoeing shed were like statues. The man with the broken arm was not wearing a gun. He was dark and tall and had very black, lank hair. His companion was a powerfully muscled, light-haired, large, thick man.

He was holding a shaping hammer in his right hand. Of the two, the man with the hammer in his hand looked most likely to be truculent, and every man in the yard had heard the exchange between the range boss and Frank Cutler.

From the main house, which was at the far southern end of the yard, someone opened and closed a door. The distance was considerable, and while the large, low residence was behind Rand Belton, Frank Cutler who was facing him had a clear view of it, even though several huge old cottonwood trees shadowed most of the front veranda. Someone had come forth to lean upon the pole railing and looked down where the strangers and Rand Belton were standing.

Frank guessed the distant person in veranda shade was the owner, so he said, "We'll wait here until you've talked to the gent over at the main house."

Belton's rugged features were gaining color and his unfriendly stare was deadly. For the second time in one day, this unwashed, unshorn, tucked-up saddle tramp he was facing had him in a position he could extricate himself from only by doing as the saddle tramp said. In front of his own men, too, and worse, in front of his employer yonder on the porch.

He turned and started walking toward the distant main house's veranda, and Frank stepped to the hitchrack to lean as he considered the pair of wooden-faced men in the barn doorway. He addressed the shorter one, a man with sloping shoulders and the steady gaze of an individual who would not take a backward step to an avalanche. "You mind telling me the name of the man over yonder with the busted arm?"

The cowboy answered shortly. "Jim."

"Thanks. Is he the one Mister Belton said could talk In'ian?"

This time the short man's answer was no less unfriendly but longer. "Yes. He's a breed 'Rapahoe. He's our wrangler."

Frank turned and started across the yard, with every eye following him. At the shoeing shed he nodded to the breed and the massive man wearing the shoeing apron. "Jim," he said to the tall man, "that old In'ian over yonder doesn't speak English. My partner and I found him in a cave. Mister Belton's got a notion he's a cattle thief. We don't think he is. I'd take it kindly if you'd tell the old man not to say anything. Not to answer any questions."

The tall breed stared a long time at Frank, then cast a sidelong glance at the big man be-

60

side him. The big man was studying Frank Cutler, heavy brows down, dark gray eyes candidly hostile. The breed cleared his throat and seemed to want to speak, but he refrained from doing so as the large man regripped his shaping hammer and said, "Who the hell do you think you are?" to Frank, then tossed the hammer backward and hunched his powerful shoulders. "If Rand figures that In'ian's a thief, then he is a thief."

Frank considered the large man. He was not wearing a gun. Clearly, he did not need weapons very often when there was an argument. Frank had made his point with the tall breed, so he turned and started back toward the hitchrack. The big man allowed him to reach the middle of the yard, then came after him.

Sam Morton stepped forward and said, "Frank!"

It was too late. The big man lunged with a ham-sized hand and half raised Frank off the ground as he swung him around. The cocked right fist was fired from shoulder height and although Frank was trying to twist away, the blow caught him under the ear. He went down with smoky vision and a silent, red-tinted explosion inside his head. He should have been knocked unconscious, but he wasn't.

Someone yelled. Frank heard that, but for moments that was all he was aware of.

Sam was coming straight ahead. The big man watched and waited. Sam was not as heavy as Frank. He was also much younger. The big man spat and waited. There was not a sound and none of the onlookers moved.

When they were within a few yards of each other Sam halted, lifted out the ivory-handled Colt and put it on the ground. The big man sneered. Sam started forward, and as the big man widened his stance and raised his oaken arms, Sam said, "You son of a bitch," and shot forward in a low crouch. At the last possible moment as the large man was starting to swing, Sam went sideways, came in from the left, and hit the big man, making him shuffle both feet in a stolid attempt to face around.

Sam never stopped moving; he favored his wounded left side as he went. The large man tried to shift often enough to be facing around, and he swung savagely into the midday air.

Sam put all he had into a belly strike and the large man's air rattled out; he bent with pain and Sam hit him squarely across the bridge of the nose. Blood sprayed. Sam stepped back and the large man tried to clear the blood from his eyes. Sam came in again, moving in a peculiar, side-winding motion. This time he hit the large man three times in the face and did not step back as the big man raised both hands.

Sam balanced backward and kicked. The big man cried out and dropped his arms. Sam took his time, aimed well, and the strike smashed flesh against jawbone. The big man fell like a tree, slowly gathering momentum all the way down.

That short rider out front of the barn started running and swearing at the same time. He was within thirty feet of Sam when Frank rolled across his old hat and cocked his six-gun with the barrel aimed at the enraged cowboy's brisket.

There was heavy, unmoving dust in the air, and there was darkening blood where the big man was lying, but there was not a sound for a long time. Not until a sharp, high voice called from back at the main house veranda.

"*Stop it!* That's enough. Jim, get a bucket of water. Carl, go back over by the barn."

The short man obeyed very slowly as Frank got to his feet, holstered his handgun, and picked up his crushed hat. His neck hurt more than his jaw. He looked at Sam, at the large man at Sam's feet, then began beating his hat against a trouser leg.

Rand Belton came striding from the veranda. When he got down there where the breed horse wrangler was upending a bucket of water over the unconscious man, he acted like someone who could not believe what he had seen. Finally, he raised his head in Frank's direction. "Go get fed at the cookshack," he said, "Take the In'ian with you. . . . And him." Belton was looking at Sam, who was tucking in his shirttail, clutching his left arm, and breathing hard.

Belton beckoned for help as he knelt to roll the large man onto his back. The man's face was ruined. Belton sent the wrangler for another bucket of water, and watched Frank and Sam as they headed for the cookhouse. Midway, they called to the old Indian, pointed at their destination, and beckoned. He scuttled toward them, his lynxlike black eyes brighter than they probably had been in many years. At the steps leading to the cookhouse porch where he caught up, the old man grinned so wide all of his pink and nearly toothless gums showed.

The cook was a product of his own capabilities. He was a man of average height who must have weighed at least two hundred and fifty pounds. Because his ankles and feet had broken down long ago, he padded around in slippers, and he breathed hard even when he did nothing more strenuous than lift the cook-shack coffeepot.

He had seen the fight from his porch. When Frank, Sam, and the Indian came inside, he made an uncertain smile and pointed. "There's hot water, gents, in case you want to wash up a little. . . . Young feller, you'd ought to soak your hands. I'll get another basin."

Sam and Frank sank down at the long table and looked at each other. Sam smiled; he had not been marred but his hands had raw knuckles and were swelling as he placed them atop the table and said, "I guess I got to watch out for you. Don't ever turn your back on someone like that."

Frank turned his head, felt grinding bones in his neck, and turned it back as he felt his jaw where the blow had landed. Tomorrow he was going to be sore as hell. "Where did you learn to fight like that?" he asked.

Sam flexed his injured hands slowly. Each movement caused pain. "I told you. I had to grow up hard."

"That man was a head taller and sixty pounds heavier, Sam. One strike and he would have torn your head off."

"Yeah, I know. Too big, Frank, and too heavy . . . I've had it like that before, a lot of times. . . . What happens when we walk out of here?"

Frank had no opportunity to answer. The cook padded over with three platters of food, then brought coffee, and the last thing he did was place a wedge of pie in front of the Indian and almost apologetically said, "That's about what a man wants who ain't got any teeth."

He then hovered as Sam and Frank began eating, clearly full of questions and curiosity, but without encouragement he lacked the boldness to speak.

The food was good. Even the coffee was fresh, which was not common on cow ranches. The Indian shoveled in the food, beginning with the pie, but he would not touch the coffee. He drank water instead. Frank glanced around once, then decided it was better not to watch the old man eat, and did not look around again.

No one intruded, but they could hear voices out in the yard, which reminded Frank that he had not answered Sam's question, so he paused to say, "I don't know what happens when we walk out of here, but I got a feeling your damned In'ian is going to be part of the family from now on, unless we can find some other In'ians who'll take him over."

Sam raised his head as the breed horse

wrangler came in, expressionless and silent as he leaned to put Sam's six-gun on the table, then straighten back gazing at the old man.

For the first time since Frank and Sam had found the old man, he spoke. His voice was reedy, sharp, terse, and the words sounded slightly guttural. He spoke rapidly to the tall breed and then leaned back waiting.

The horse wrangler eyed Frank before replying. He spoke slowly and to no great length, then shot Frank another glance and switched to English. "I done like you said, mister. I told him not to answer no questions or nothing. . . . His name is Plume. That's sort of like Smith. His clan's gone to the mountains to make meat."

"And they left him in the cave to die."

The breed nodded. "He can't ride no more and he gets sick easy. He's old an' worn out."

Sam looked around at the man with the broken arm. "How'd you get hurt?"

"Horse fell with me. It's healin' good though."

"Your name is Jim?"

"Yes. Jim."

"Jim, who was that big son of a bitch?"

Jim required no more description than that. "Jack Schmidt. He's hurt real bad. They got to take him to the doctor over at Fort Mc-

Call. That's two days over and two days back." Jim did not take his dark eyes with their muddy whites off Sam Morton all the time he was speaking, and even afterward, until someone shouted out in the yard when he left the cookhouse.

CHAPTER 6

Skye

Sam had a cud in his cheek and Frank was lighting a cigarette when the door opened again, but this time the person who entered did so slowly.

Frank did not look up because he was getting the quirley fired up, but Sam did. So did the cook over at his stove. He immediately wiped both palms upon his flour-sack apron and went after a clean cup to fill with coffee.

Frank finally felt more than saw that something different was at hand, and he turned. It was a woman. She was not tall and she was not willowy. But everywhere Frank looked, she was woman. She had curly dark hair, green eyes, strong arms, and strong, tanned hands.

She came to the table, waited until the cook had placed the cup down, then sat and without a word studied first Sam, then Frank. Finally, she glanced at the old Indian, who returned her gaze with his sharp stare.

She pushed the cup aside and said, "Rand told me about you two. You'll be Mister Cutler?"

Frank inclined his head. She had a complexion of soft gold and white. Her nose tipped up slightly and the green eyes were large and set well back. He did not make a conscious effort to guess her age but thought she was in her twenties. She was wearing a checked cotton blouse which fit loosely everywhere except where it couldn't. Frank put down the cigarette.

She said, "I'm Skye Cameron," and they both stared; it had never once occurred to either of them that Skye Cameron was not a man.

She swung her glance to the old Indian. For a long time they looked at one another, then she spoke again. "This is Plume, in case you didn't know. He has six sons. They shoot cattle, occasionally steal them, and now and then raid my horse herd at night."

Frank did not take his eyes off her, but Sam shot the old Indian a troubled look. "Ma'am," Sam said, "he's as old as the hills."

She accepted the sound of protest in Sam's words. "Yes, he is old, but his sons are not and he taught them to hate whites." She looked at Sam. "You found an old man who had been left to starve to death and wanted to help him. I appreciate that, Mister Morton."

Sam was not finished. "Belton was after him. All you've got to do is look at him. He didn't steal any cattle."

Skye Cameron's gaze, showing irony, drifted back to Frank Cutler. "He's stolen more cattle and horses in his time than most people will ever own, and he has been the enemy of whites all his life. . . . You should have left him in the cave."

Frank inclined his head a little. "Yes'm, but not after your foreman came up there."

"Why not, Mister Cutler?"

"Because the old bronco is feeble and Belton said he knew ways to make him talk. He'd have killed him, ma'am." At the steady look he was getting, Frank shifted a little on the bench, then also said, "In'ians don't mean anything to me, ma'am, but since I was a button I've had no use for bullies, and even less use for someone who would beat up on a feeble old man, no matter what color his hide is."

Skye Cameron softly said, "That's admirable, Mister Cutler. I don't like bullies either, but I like losing livestock every year a lot less." She paused before finishing. "This old man has been nothing but trouble for more than fifty years. Everyone within five hundred miles of my yard has had trouble with him."

Frank did not yield. "But not for some time, ma'am. How much time does he have left? Maybe a year, two years at the best. . . . Like I said to your range boss, if you got In'ian trouble, bring in the army."

The still, large, green eyes appeared to be looking through Frank. He was not going to give an inch. She said, "What will you do with him? You only have two horses. Can he stand riding for days on end?"

Frank had no ready answer because right from the start he had not thought in those terms. "Maybe find some In'ians and hand him over to them."

Skye Cameron faintly smiled. "He belongs to a clan who have gone north to make meat. Do you know anything about Arapahoes, Mister Cutler? No other clan will take him — *especially* him."

Sam interrupted. "Then he'll go along with us. I'll tell you one thing, ma'am, we won't leave him here for Mister Belton to beat on."

Skye Cameron studied young Sam Morton in a calm, almost pensive way, then she smiled at him. It was a nicer smile than the one she had showed Frank. It was probably a much safer smile, too, because Sam was younger than she was, and Frank was not. "You broke the nose and jaw of one of my best riders, Mister Morton."

Sam blinked, thrown off because she changed the subject. He reddened. "Well, it wasn't my doing, ma'am. He came up onto Frank from behind."

She finally reached for the coffee cup and for as long as she raised it and drank, Cutler and Morton gazed at her in silence. Then she put the cup down and said, "Your horses have been fed and grained. You've been fed." She stood up no longer smiling. "Be out of the yard within an hour — and take Plume with you."

Then she strode out of the cookhouse.

The cook audibly sighed, saw Sam looking at him, and shrugged shoulders layered with fat. "You're lucky, gents. I've seen her peel the hide off a man with her tongue — without ever touching him."

Sam scowled. "Why doesn't her husband do a little peeling on his own?"

"She don't have a husband. She almost had one. I rode for her old pappy back then. He died. She took to a feller named Jackson. He rode for the old man too. . . . He went lookin' for bulls one day and never come back. . . . They never found him. . . . It was In'ians sure as hell."

The cook lumbered over to refill their coffee cups. Frank punched out his smoke and said, "That's it. That's why she don't like In'ians."

The cook leaned on the table breathing hard. "Maybe. I said her pappy died. He did. Seven years after In'ians shot a arrowpoint into his spine. He couldn't sleep on his back and he couldn't stand ridin' in a wagon or buggy, and he couldn't even set straight in a chair. . . . Seven damned years of livin' like that. . . . How would you feel about In'ians, mister?"

Sam silently and slowly reached for his refilled cup. Frank glanced in the direction of the door through which the handsome woman had passed.

The cook was padding back toward his cookstove with the big pot when he also said, "Gents, I seen the fight in the yard and all, but let me tell you somethin' else. You're downright lucky. Skye Cameron's a spit 'n' image of her old pappy. Neither one of you would have rode out of this yard if that had been him over yonder on the porch, no matter what it took. And she's just as hard, except that I guess she thinks different, being female and all. But I'd do like she said — be gone before the hour is out."

Frank arose, reached inside his shirt to scratch, then dropped a glance to Sam and jerked his head. They went out into the yard where the slanting sunrays were being blocked by the big log barn, with old Plume padding in their wake.

There was only one Cameron rider in sight. He was sitting on a tipped-back chair over on the porch of the bunkhouse; and although he had certainly seen them leave the cookhouse, he continued to gaze straight ahead from beneath the tipped down brim of his hat.

They rigged out inside the barn without a word passing between them, led their animals out back, and swung up. The day was getting well along toward its end as they turned northward in the direction of some very distant mountains. Old Plume, behind Sam's cantle and clutching Sam's belt, made some little clucking sounds that could have been laughter.

The land looked flat from the ranch yard, but it rolled and dipped. There was a dogleg bend with green willows along it where that white-water little creek ran, the same creek that also passed behind the Cameron ranch yard. Frank picked a good site, about five miles from the yard, and meandered over to it; then he dismounted and looked up at Sam.

"We should have brought something with us for breakfast."

Sam waited until Plume had slid down, then he swung his leg over and came to the ground looking irritable. "Yeah. They'd have put strychnine in it."

Sam lingered a long time at the creek soaking his swollen hands. Frank found a suitable spot for his bedroll and turned to find the old Indian watching him. He reddened, pulled out one of his blankets, and tossed it over. The old man's gums showed as he clutched the blanket, and when Sam returned Frank said, "We got to do something about the old man. I got one blanket left, and one's never been enough."

They built a small fire and Frank bedded down as close to it as he dared. He also piled an armload of twigs nearby so that when he awakened during the night, cold to the bone, he'd have something to get the fire hot again.

At least the horses were perfectly content. Feed was fetlock high and rich.

CHAPTER 7

A Problem

Dawn arrived. They were out of sight of the ranch yard, in a country so silently immense that there was no room for sound. The landscape was reduced to its essentials: surface, horizon, and sky.

And their horses were gone.

Frank stood up in his bare feet, mindless of the cold, moving his eyes slowly in all directions. There was nothing out there but what had always been there, and no horses. He turned, gazing bitterly at the flattened grass where his blanket had been. It, and the old Indian, were also gone.

He lightly kicked the feet of his companion, and when Sam's shock of hair came up, Frank said, "We're afoot."

Sam sat up rubbing his eyes, then he spat and turned his head slowly. By the time he was ready to roll out and reach for his boots, Frank was hunched over stoically kindling a fire.

Sam went to the creek and returned. Frank offered a tin cup of hot coffee, which was all they had, and when their eyes met Frank said, "She was right, Sam. That old man was a first-class son of a bitch."

Sam drank, sat close to the fire, and was silent for a long time. When he had finished his coffee he arose and without speaking went out where the horses had been hobbled; he remained out there until the sun arrived, then he returned and tossed down their hobbles. "And after all we did for him," he said.

"I didn't think he had the strength, Sam."

"He didn't, Frank. There were three of them who rode down from the northeast on barefoot horses. Maybe as the lady said, it was his sons. Whoever it was took him with them."

Frank used grass to swipe out his tin cup, then he methodically rolled his first smoke of the day. "Well, I'll tell you how I feel, Sam. I broke that *grulla* horse when he was three. We been over a lot of country together. I'm going to get him back."

Sam felt especially bad because he had insisted that they take care of the Indian. He scratched, fed more twigs into the little fire, and raised his head only when he heard something down the creek southward.

Instead of being elated at what he saw, Sam swore. "Goddamn. Look yonder, Frank."

It was Skye Cameron with four riders. They were approaching slowly, still bundled against the earlier cold.

When they drew rein in silence, Frank and Sam arose facing them. Skye was wearing a hat of beaver belly color. She did not smile as she said, "Good morning. I thought you'd be farther along than this. . . . Where is Plume?"

Frank reddened. "He isn't here."

The green eyes studied Frank. "Neither are your horses, Mister Cutler."

Frank's color deepened. He looked steadily up at her. "Yes'm, the horses are gone too."

Skye turned her head. "Carl, see what you can find."

That sloping-shouldered man turned impassively aside. Another rider accompanied him. Skye leaned both hands atop her saddle horn looking down. Frank knew what was coming, and while the idea irritated him, there was no answer.

She said, "I told you I admired your concern for the old man, and I did, Mister Cutler. You just don't happen to be a good judge of human nature, so now he's gone with your horses."

Frank glared at the grass. He could not tell her to get the hell out of his sight because they were standing on her land, but he would have liked to say something like that, and Sam did get short with her.

"If we'd left him with you, ma'am, he'd likely be dead by now."

Carl returned and reported. "Three In'ians. They come from up yonder and to the east, and they went west from here. Three barefoot horses and two wearin' shoes."

Skye nodded. "How long ago?"

"Maybe about midnight last night — a long start, ma'am."

"West, Carl? Plume's clan is in the north-ward mountains."

The short man shrugged. "Likely they figured someone would try to track them, and they didn't want to lead no one to their rancheria."

The other rider spoke. He was a stocky man. Neither Frank nor Sam had seen him before. "Didn't have to be anyone the old In'ian knew, Miss Cameron. I'd say most likely it wasn't, because as near as I can figure, they wasn't following these two fellers. They come straight down from the northeast. . . . I'd say they seen a fire out here, knew there would be horses, and stoled them after these fellers was bedded down."

Frank and Sam listened to the stocky man. He did not sound like a man making a guess. Carl looped his reins and started a cigarette. He refused to look at the men on foot. One of them, the older one, had come within an ace of shooting him in the brisket the day before, and Carl was not a man who forgave very readily.

Skye Cameron gazed off to her left. There was nothing but open grassland as far as a person could see, until blue-hazed, distant mountains merged darkly with the flawless morning sky. She said, "Barefoot horses?" and both Carl and the stocky man nodded their answer. She was puzzled about something.

Eventually she spoke to Carl again, acting as though Frank and Sam did not exist. "In'ians might ride west for a ways, but they wouldn't stay in open country, Carl." She raised her hand with the rein in it. "Let's shag them a ways."

Carl's face showed annoyance. "We figured to find the sore-footed bulls, ma'am."

Her reply was almost casual. "All right. Take everyone but Mack and keep looking for them. Mack, you ride with me. We'll be back before evening, Carl."

The short man's expression of annoyance deepened, but as he raised his hand and jerked his head for the other men to ride with him, he said nothing more.

When only Skye and the man she had called Mack were alone with Frank and Sam, she looked down. "Walk back to the yard. Homer will feed you and when I get back maybe there will be something to tell you. At least we'll know more than we do now."

Sam watched them ride out where the horses had been hobbled the night before and said, "That damned female can't open her mouth without ordering someone around. . . . You going to walk back like she said?"

Frank was watching and did not answer right away. "Well, you got another suggestion? No horses, no food . . . "

Sam raised his face and squinted at the rising sun. Heat was on the way but it would not arrive for another hour or so. He lowered his head. Skye Cameron and her rider were quartering. The stocky man seemed knowledgeable. He halted and gestured with an upraised arm, and Skye Cameron appeared to be listening to whatever he was saying.

Sam said, "That damned old man," and

Frank slapped him roughly on the shoulder. "If we'd been fifty miles farther out it would have been a hell of a lot different. Let's go."

They hung their outfits as high as possible among the creek willows. If they had not, by the time they got back salt-starved varmints would have chewed half the leather off.

Then they started walking. Five miles was not a great distance, except to men who were unaccustomed to walking distances. By the time they had rooftops in sight Sam had a blistered heel and Frank's hunger bothered him. When Sam said, "This here is like crawlin' back," Frank's answer was curt. "Partner, you remember this: survival is your sixth sense. When we rode out of Powell, you left the other five back there. Eating crow is better than eating nothing."

Sam limped along, eyeing the yonder heat-warped distance. "They won't find our horses." He trudged awhile, then also said, "Yeah, you're right. Anyway, she'll sell us two more."

No one was in the yard when they entered it. The entire area looked and felt deserted. They went to the stone trough, drank, and sluiced off. Then they went over to the cook-house and found the *cocinero* sitting out back barefooted, cocked back in a chair in the shade of the overhang roof, sipping watered whiskey, and sweating like a stud horse.

He was so surprised at their appearance that his mouth opened and no sound came forth. Then he rocked forward and wheezingly leaned to put his whiskey glass out of sight behind a kindling box.

Frank sank down on the steps, removed his hat, and wiped off sweat. Sam was tugging off one of his boots. The cook finally found his voice. "Where'd you two come from? By now you should have been — "

Sam said, "Frank, did you ever see a blister that big?"

Frank smiled at the cook. "Homer. That's what the lady said your name was. Homer, we're as hungry as a pair of bitch wolves."

The cook was eyeing Sam's naked and upraised foot. He started to heave up out of the chair as he spoke. "I got some salt an' bakin' soda. You don't want no infection to start. I'll fetch you a basin of hot water with them medicines in it." He padded in the direction of the door as though he had not heard anything Frank had said.

Sam lowered the naked foot and wiggled his toes in the sunlight. "I don't like being here, I don't like that danged woman, and this is the first time I been afoot since I was nine years old. . . . Frank, you're a jinx."

For a moment Frank's hands, which were working like spiders fashioning a brown-paper smoke, stopped dead still. Then they started moving again. He lit up, blew smoke, and glanced around the big, hardpan yard. "After we eat, we better go out back where that trough is and bathe. I been itching ever since we were in that cave. I knew that'd happen."

"Knew what would happen?"

"Fleas. Any time you find a cave where animals have denned up, there are fleas."

Homer returned with the basin. When Sam lowered his foot he winced. The water was hot. Homer grunted downward to sift in salt and baking soda, then he reached for the railing to help himself in straightening up. "I got a fire going under the grub," he told them. "Now tell me — how come you two come back?"

Frank sighed. "Because your boss met us in camp and told us to. She said you'd feed us."

"Is that a fact? Why would she do a thing like that?"

Frank avoided looking at Homer. "Because last night some sons of bitches stole our horses. That's why."

Homer considered that a long while before

asking one more question. "Where's the old In'ian?"

Sam raised his dripping foot and regarded it. There was more pink color to it than the foot had had since he'd been a baby. "The old In'ian," he stated very slowly, "went with our horses, and now you know the whole story. . . . How is that meal coming?"

Homer padded inside but left the door ajar. Frank smoked, looked far out, and felt drowsy as the increasing heat worked on him. "Jinx," he murmured. "Jinx! You darned ingrate."

Sam laughed. "How much money we got, Frank? She's not going to *give* us no horses."

Frank did not say how much money he had, but there was enough.

Two horsemen walking their horses entered the yard from the west, over behind the barn. They were talking as they swung off and led the animals inside to the saddle pole before stripping them. Sam leaned to see who it was, but they were inside the barn by then, so he leaned back and delved through several pockets to find his chewing tobacco.

Frank had made no effort to see who the riders were because he recognized their voices. One was Rand Belton. The other man was that tall, lean rider someone had called

Fred, the man who had stood in front of the barn with Carl, unable to make up his mind what he should do when trouble started.

They heard the front door slam and Sam raised his eyes. Frank shrugged. "The fat old bastard probably don't get much chance to be important. Anyway, they'd see us sooner or later."

He was correct. When they filed inside to eat, Rand and the tall man were already at the table. They looked up. Rand did not nod but Fred did.

Homer dished up platters and put them on the table, then he went for the coffeepot. Not a word was spoken until Rand finally put down his eating tools and said, "Some folks live and learn, and some folks just live. She told you about that damned old bronco."

Sam's head came up fast but Frank nudged him and went right on eating. Sam glared but heeded the nudge and went back to his meal.

Fred was uncomfortable. He ate fast, finished first, and went after another cup of java. He and Homer exchanged a look, then Fred went back to sit down. The atmosphere inside the cookhouse was hostile. Rand pushed his plate back and pulled his cup in close; he watched Frank and Sam for a while before speaking again.

"Are they lookin' for your horses?"

Frank nodded.

Rand sat in silence for a moment before he spoke again. "We had to send the breed and the wagon up to Fort McCall with that feller you hurt yesterday." He let that lie for a moment. "That makes us shorthanded by two. This is a poor time to be shorthanded. We got a gather to make to cull down. We got some damned bulls with sore feet standing in mud somewhere instead of covering cows. And we got three hunnert first-calf heifers to watch." Rand drank coffee and shoved the cup away before speaking again. "You fellers made us all kinds of trouble yesterday."

Frank was finished and leaned on the scarred old table looking down at the range boss. "When you get through moaning," he said, "say what's on your mind."

Rand's jaw muscles rippled as he watched Homer refill his cup. "We need two more riders," he said, pulling the refilled cup close. "Cameron ranch ain't like some, close enough to a town so's someone can ride in and hire men."

"Otherwise you wouldn't want us," said Frank. He looked at Sam. "It's up to you."

For a while Sam continued to swipe around his plate to soak up the last of the gravy with a bit of bread. Finally he said, "This is your loafing year, Frank. Anyway, I don't care much for the range boss, or the lady he works for, but Homer is a good cook."

Fred intently drank his coffee and avoided looking at any of them. Over at the stove, Homer raised a soiled sleeve to rid his face and neck of sweat and kept his back to the table.

Rand Belton shook his head and leaned as though to arise, his dark eyes sardonic rather than angry or insulted. "You know something, gents? You both got up on the wrong side of life. You don't listen, you don't learn, you don't belong, and most likely neither one of you are worth a damn in the saddle neither."

Sam was on his feet as the range boss finished. Belton was leaning on the table as their eyes met. He did not appear fearful, although it had to be still vivid in his mind what an angry Sam Morton could do.

"I'll tell you something else, gents," he said, holding Sam's glare. "You're as close to nowhere as it's possible to get, and, without horses, by the time you reach a town by walkin' your clothes will be out of style."

Belton left the cookhouse by the front door. Fred followed shortly after, wearing a feeble smile. Frank turned slowly toward Homer. "What did he mean?"

Homer used a towel this time to mop off sweat. "I expect he meant they ain't going to sell you boys no horses. . . . Unless maybe you help out a little with the work." Homer paused to wheeze a moment. "Listen, boys; it's a good outfit. No matter what you think of him — or her — it's a good outfit. . . . Maybe a little tough, but after all we're in the middle of nowhere without even any neighbors." Homer tossed down the limp towel and balanced a final thought for a while before putting it into words. And then, his voice was quaking with uncertainty because he, too, knew what kind of men he was addressing.

"I'm a sight older than either of you. I seen lots of 'em come and go. . . . Now don't take no offense at this. You fellers was wrong a lot. It never hurts to be wrong as long as a man can admit it. You was wrong as hell about that old bronco. And about Miz Cameron, an' about Rand. . . . I don't mean no offense. It's just that I've seen a lot of men come and go; seen a lot of 'em be wrong without the guts to admit it, an' they went from wrong to wrong. . . . That's all."

Frank and Sam sat a long time gazing at the cook. When they finally rose to leave the cookhouse, Frank went over and slapped Homer's shoulder. Then he followed Sam outside where Sam had left his boot and his sock with the big hole in the heel.

CHAPTER 8

A Death

They did not see the range boss again, but while they were dressing after bathing at the stone trough, Fred ambled out back from the barn and leaned on a corral stringer, looking friendly. When Frank said, "That damned water is colder'n a snow bank," Fred grinned.

"We sluice off in the creek; it's warmer. Did Homer give you some soap?"

Sam held up what remained of a chunk of something thick and brown. His blister had broken and the soap, which had potash and lye in it, had burned. "What do you fellers put in this stuff — wolf poison?"

Fred fished in a back pocket and held up a worn but clean pair of socks. He said, "I seen yours at the cookshack. They get a hole in 'em and if a man's got to walk very much that'll make a blister every time. . . . Go ahead, take 'em. I got three pairs."

They were still cold after dressing but the sun was hot so they remained back there as still as lizards, soaking up heat. Fred rambled on about the ranch, the work, the weather. He was a good-natured man, and perhaps he was also wiser than he appeared to be, because he did not mention the fight in the yard yesterday or their misfortune last night up along the creek.

By the time he ambled toward the barn because it was getting close to chore time, Frank and Sam had heard a number of things that coincided with what the cook had told them.

Frank tipped down his hat to keep sunlight from his eyes and said, "I don't like to be wrong. . . . I remember being wrong once before, when I was eight years old." He turned calm, sardonic eyes upon Sam Morton. The younger man was perching upon the edge of the old trough, favoring his sore foot. He missed the dry humor because he was occupied with private, and bitter, thoughts. Eventually he said, "You know, Frank, I grew up dislikin' certain kinds of people. A man does something to help folks, and they turn around and do something mean to him, like stealing his horse."

"Anybody who is as big as Homer is got to

be right now and then, Sam."

"What's big got to do with it?"

"Nothing . . . He was right."

"Yeah." Sam looked at Frank. "Once before, when you were eight years old!"

Frank laughed, shoved back his hat and straightened up. He was ready to also go over to the barn when something caught his eye. He waited a long time, then quietly said, "Sam, she found something. Look."

The riders were more than a mile out, and if the sun had not been slanting away on its downward course which created shadows and less brilliance, they might have been able to see things better.

"They're leading horses, Sam."

Something did not look right to Frank. He stared in the direction of the barn, walking up through without seeing Fred in the shadows, or looking around to see if Sam was limping in his wake.

Out front at the hitchrack he leaned and squinted. They were closer and he finally was able to see that Skye and Mack were moving very slowly because the horses they were leading could move no faster. He saw something else; one of the horses had a burden on its back.

Fred emerged from the barn, looked northward, stared, then went hurrying in the direction of the bunkhouse. Moments later Rand returned to the front of the barn with Fred.

They reached the yard and walked steadily toward the silent and waiting men. Skye tossed a lead shank to Fred and dismounted. She looked straight at Frank, who walked around the rack and stood gazing at the dead man tied belly-down across one of the weak, tucked up horses.

Sam limped over there too. After a moment he turned toward Skye Cameron. "He's been shot."

She allowed Rand to take her reins, "Yes. We came onto him about ten miles west. . . . I can't understand why they would take him along, then shoot him, unless they didn't want to shoot him last night near your camp because it would awaken both of you." She pulled off her roping gloves and watched Sam for a moment. From twenty feet away she could see the big vein in the side of Sam's neck pulse hard. She had her own idea why old Plume had been out there last night, when those horse thieves had arrived — because he had intended to steal their horses himself — but she had no intention of mentioning this now. Maybe never.

Frank turned slowly toward her. "What's

the rest of it, ma'am."

"Well, for one thing they weren't In'ians, Mister Cutler. For another thing — look at those horses. They've been ridden almost to death. They had shoes once, not too long ago. Mack thinks the men pulled them off because the range has lots of barefoot horses and they'd be harder to track. Impossible to track, in fact, riding barefoot animals."

Mack returned from out back where he had filled up on water. He had sweat running under his shirt and dripping from his chin. Leaning on the rack eyeing Frank and Sam, he quietly said, "Outlaws, not redskins. It was them bare hooves that made me think first off that it was In'ians. . . . It was outlaws sure as I'm standing here. I think it was lucky for you fellers that you wasn't out there last night too. They'd have murdered you. . . . We found the old In'ian where they'd had a camp. Looked like maybe they'd spent a lot of time at that camp. Maybe until the sun was up this morning. Then they cut north toward the mountains."

There were riders coming from the northeast, but no one heeded them until they reached the yard, by which time Sam, Fred, and Rand had lifted the dead Indian down and had carried him inside the barn where it was cooler.

Skye Cameron went to the main house and did not reappear until the sun was gone, and everything Mack knew or could surmise had been told and dissected by the men on the porch of the bunkhouse.

Carl had found the sore-footed bulls, as he had thought he might, standing to their hocks in creek side mud to alleviate the fever in their feet. That was one problem about importing up-bred bulls: they had been raised in meadows on grass and soft earth, and walking five or ten miles every few days to find a cow or heifer to cover got them tender-footed. That meant fever. Instinct told them what to do and they did it.

He borrowed Sam's plug and was returning it when Mack said, "I figure it like this. There's three of them bastards, but they got only two fresh horses. That means one of 'em is still ridin' a worn down animal."

Carl spat past the railing. "They'll leave him or slow down to his gait."

Mack nodded.

Carl spat again. "They won't leave him. Why should they? Whatever they done, they done it a hell of a long way from here, and if anyone was chasin' them they'd have been able to see that long before now in this open country. So they got nothing to worry about, except to keep moving maybe."

Frank had been listening for a half hour without speaking. Now he said, "If that's so and they slow down, Sam and I can catch up, maybe."

The men turned to look at Frank, without any of them speaking. Someone was coming down the yard through soft dusk, and across the yard Homer came out to ring his triangle, summoning the riders to supper. Rand led off, the others followed until only Sam and Frank were left, and Frank was studying the approaching silhouette when he said, "Go ahead, partner. I'll be along directly."

Sam looked at the silhouette, recognized Skye Cameron, leaned to softly say, "Make sure they're damned good horses, Frank," then he went limping in the direction of the lighted cookhouse.

She halted just beyond the porch overhang, without speaking or nodding, and looked directly at Frank. She was wearing a blouse that looked creamy-colored in the poor light but actually was white. Her riding trousers with their buckskin lining on the inside of each leg were clean, and the scuffed boots she had been wearing earlier had been replaced with a newer pair.

He said, "My partner and I would like to

buy a couple of good horses, ma'am."

She nodded gently as she moved closer to the porch railing. "I'm sorry we couldn't get your horses back, Mister Cutler."

"Best thing that you didn't find them, ma'am. Sam and I'll do that. That *grulla* horse is an old friend of mine."

She looked up at him. "Mack is sure they went north into the mountains."

"So he said."

"Can you read sign, Mister Cutler?"

Frank returned her gaze. He could follow a cow from a water hole with mud on her feet and that was about all. He had no intention of confessing his inadequacy so he said, "Three riders leave a lot of sign, Miss Cameron."

"Not once they get into the mountains, Mister Cutler. Unless they ride over game trails. When I was a girl my father and I tracked cattle and wolves in the foothills, sometimes in the mountains too. He could read sign as well as any In'ian." She leaned on the railing, profiled to him, looking in the direction of the lighted cookhouse. "I wish I knew where old Plume's people are up there. But we could never find them in time." She turned slowly toward him again. "I have a ranch cemetery out a ways. My parents and several riders are buried out there. . . . Mister

Cutler, dead people are neither right nor wrong, are they?"

He smiled gently. "Nor red or white . . . I saw the cemetery the day we rode in the first time. . . . I didn't think you'd do it. You hated that old In'ian."

She did not deny his charge but she said, "Plume was trapped. He was part of the early days, of history. He should have died long ago, but he couldn't; he was trapped by history. I'm sure he knew a lot of suffering, and I'm sure he's glad it's over. . . . Maybe you can explain that to your partner before he does something he'll regret."

"Such as, ma'am?"

"He wanted to protect old Plume. The look on his face when he was standing there looking at the dead old man belly-down across the horse . . . If Sam ever finds the man who killed Plume, it wouldn't have to be a fair fight. He'd kill him like he'd kill a rattler."

Frank leaned on the railing looking at her. Eventually he smiled. Homer was so damned right. "If you'll sell us a couple of good, stout horses, we'll ride on tomorrow. . . . I want to tell you something, Miss Cameron. . . . I've never been so darned wrong about someone before in my life. Sam and me both."

She matched his faint smile. "Nor I, Mister

Cutler . . . I'll have Rand bring in some horses first thing in the morning. You take your pick. Ten dollars a head."

He straightened up to tell her that any broken horse in the world was worth at least three times that much money, but she turned and walked back in the direction of the main house, leaving him standing there.

CHAPTER 9

Three Man Hunters

Rand was his usual peremptory self when Carl, Fred, and Mack slammed the gate closed amid dun dust, and the horses they had brought in were milling, snorting, and acting as though they had never seen the inside of a corral before.

He did not ask Frank or Sam what they liked. He pointed first to a rawboned big bay with a good head and powerful forelegs, and said, "Jim broke that horse two years ago, an' I rode him most of last summer. He's got more power and bottom than any horse you've ever ridden." Having said that, Rand squinted through the thinning dust and pointed again, this time toward a short-backed, slightly pigeon-toed, light bay with a mule nose and large eyes that were slightly slanted. "Tough, businesslike, a mite spooky,

102

solid as stone, and you can't wear him out. He's seven. The big horse is five."

Rand turned, and having made the selection for Sam and Frank, waited for one of them to speak. They didn't speak; they leaned and studied all the horses. Rand waited, then turned away tugging at his droopy moustache.

Finally, Frank said, "Those two, Rand."

The range boss turned back nodding his head. "Carl, fetch them over to the barn."

Sam had a question. "Can they be ridden bareback? Our outfits are in the trees up where we was camped."

Rand's flinty eyes brightened. "We'll find out, won't we? But we got extra outfits in the barn if you don't want to try barebacking them."

Frank and Sam took the horses up through the barn, turned them several times, led them around a little, then went back and accepted the bridles Mack offered them. Everyone stood back to watch, and without any question hoped there would be some fireworks, but there were none. The big bay spread his legs to keep a good balance as Frank climbed onto his back and waited for whatever Frank asked him to do. He was perfectly tractable.

The mule-nosed horse was fidgety, but

Sam sprang up and settled lightly. The mule-nosed horse bunched up a little, not to pitch but rather to be instantly ready to obey a command. But he was not a calm animal. He was one of those horses with nerves near the surface; as long as nothing went wrong, he would do everything asked of him to the best of his ability. He was also one of those horses that if a man ever got hung up in a stirrup, he would drag him to death. But that was why range men wore high enough heels on their boots so a foot would not go completely through a stirrup. It was also the reason range men shook their heads over the Mexican custom of riding steel, rather than wood, stirrups.

When Frank and Sam reined up to the hitchrack, Mack, who had been fidgeting about something, came boldly up and said, "I don't know how good you fellers are at reading sign, but I've been doin' it a long time. I could get a few days off and ride along."

Rand was standing back along the log wall scowling, and Frank noticed this. "The outfit is shorthanded," he told the stocky man and then raised his eyes to the range boss. "We'll hire on when we come back, if the jobs are still open."

Belton's scowl did not lift. "*If* you come back, they'll be open. There's no one else around."

Homer came wheezing from the cookhouse with two bundles wrapped in flour sacking. "Grub," he announced, handing up the bundles. "Be almighty careful."

They thanked Homer and reined out of the yard on their bareback horses, heading for the upper reaches of the creek where their outfits were waiting. The morning was turning warm, but there was a breathless, somewhat heavy atmosphere which made Frank study the sky.

One of those high, partially transparent veils of obscure mistiness was advancing from the northeast. It did not have to presage rain, but it certainly meant a change was on the way.

When they reached the campsite two porcupines were sluggishly trying to get up where the salt-impregnated saddle leather was. They had probably been trying since the day before, but their body weight bent the slim willow branches. They ignored Frank and Sam, whined almost constantly, and occasionally fell, only to roll over and waddle back to try again.

Sam shook his head as he and Frank dismounted. He went over, shook both creatures out of the willows, and used a stick to herd them away. They did not offer a fight, or flee.

Dim-witted as they were, they feared nothing, not even from the most innovative and deadly animal alive, the one who walked on only two legs. They waddled on their way, complaining bitterly. When Sam went back, Frank was rigging out and grinning. "They remind you of anyone?" he asked.

Sam shook his head.

"Rand. Stubborn, never laughs, complains a lot."

Frank finished first and turned the raw-boned big bay a couple of times while Sam was settling his saddle and facing away as he worked. Frank quietly said, "Damn it."

Sam turned inquiringly and saw the rider approaching from southward along the creek. His mouth fell open. The rider had a booted carbine, a bedroll, a coat atop the bedroll, and full saddlebags. The rider was also wearing a handsome beaver belly hat.

When she was close and had reined to a stop, Frank stared disapprovingly, and Skye said, "I don't think either one of you can track an elephant through a snowfield."

There were a number of things for Frank to say. He met her green-eyed gaze and did not say any of them until he was shortening the reins to pull his horse close to be mounted. Then all he said was, "Sam," and the younger man, also speechless, looked from Frank to Skye Cameron and led his horse back and forth a few times before mounting him.

They were leaving the creek after splashing across it on a northwesterly course when she spoke to them both very matter-of-factly. "We won't bother tracking them. I know where to cut the sign without riding all the way over where they had their camp. It will save half a day."

Sam finally spoke to her. "This ain't any business for a lady."

The green eyes rested thoughtfully for a moment upon Sam Morton before she answered him. "It's no business for greenhorns, either."

Sam blinked, then began to redden.

Skye gave him no chance. She gestured with a gloved hand. "You don't know this country or those mountains. I do. Every mile of them. Sam . . . Rand told me you both agreed to hire on. . . . You work for me."

He might have accepted the first of what she had said, grudgingly, but his eyes flashed over the last of it. "Lady, I quit," he told her. "I never in my life rode for a woman, and I've heard plenty from fellers who have, and I don't ever — "

"All right. You quit. . . . Sam, is there

107

something awful about one person wanting to help another person?"

Frank rode in obvious discomfort. He did not like this but could not for the life of him think of any way to stop it.

Skye was not finished. "There are rancherias up in there," she told them, looking toward the faraway foothills with their backdrop mountains. "This time of year the In'ians hunt those mountains and make meat for winter." She paused for a long moment, gazing steadily into the distance as though a thought had occurred to her that she could not easily rid herself of. Then she briskly said, "You'd be forever riding around up there, Sam, and those men would be getting farther away."

Sam slouched along for a few yards and finally said, "Well, I can't talk for Frank, but to me it don't look seemly for a woman to be riding along on a manhunt." Then he lapsed into a surly silence.

Frank rolled and lit a smoke, looked from one of them to the other, trickled smoke, and concentrated on the distance they had to cover — which was considerable. He also thought of the possibility of those outlaws sitting up there somewhere, probably in a camp where they could look back down across the open country, watching three riders heading in their direction. Without ever having seen it happen, he knew for a fact that many people had been ambushed and rolled down into deep canyons where they had never been found.

The sun climbed, time passed; they were riding across a huge expanse of open country where the mountains never seemed to get closer no matter how long a person rode toward them. Frank finally turned and said, "It's big."

She nodded, her eyes still, her features composed. "I've ridden out here many times and sat quiet looking at it. How can anything so still and silent and empty, so unchanging and timeless, have so many secrets and such endless activity?" She smiled at Frank.

The sun was changing color and soft shadows were inching southward from the nearing foothills before she led them to a creek where dozens of nesting birds rose up in panic, shrieking and scolding, as they swung off to loosen cinches and remove bridles so their horses could drink.

The mountains were still a fair distance in front. Behind them there was yet sunshine. Ahead of them the timbered uplands which were upended and crumpled for several hundred miles were already dark, but then except for glades and old burns, full sunlight never reached the ground up there.

They ate while the watered horses cropped grass. Sam went up along the creek out of sight and Frank said, "When I was his age I was about the same."

She was interested. "Have you been partners very long?"

Frank did not want her to do much rummaging in this area because it might lead back to Powell, so all he said was, "Couple of months is all. But I know him pretty well, Miz Cameron. Give him time."

She settled her shoulders against a small white oak which had bear claw scratches on it. "You never had children, Mister Cutler?"

He looked up, startled.

"I mean, since I've known both of you, it's seemed that he listens to you like a father, and you guide him like a son."

Frank lifted his hat, scratched, and reset it. Then he looked over his shoulder but there was no sign of Sam, so he looked farther, toward the mountains, and spoke to her without facing back around.

"Could they get up across those rims?"

She watched his profile for a moment, then accepted the fact that he had not liked the direction of their conversation and replied briskly. "They probably could — but not with one of them riding a worn-down, barefoot horse. And it would be hard riding. I think they will turn off, probably westerly, and keep to the timber while heading in that direction. They wouldn't turn eastward, would they? That's the direction they came from. They did something over there bad enough to make them run in the opposite direction."

Frank faced forward again, saw her eyes thoughtfully regarding him, and said, "Suppose they run into broncos?"

A dark shadow seemed to pass slowly across her eyes before she replied. "It has happened up there, Mister Cutler. But generally, I don't think anything bad would happen. Providing they didn't bring it upon themselves. . . . I've known many In'ians . . ."

"Did you ever know one you liked, ma'am?"

The green eyes showed quick resentment. "I'm not an In'ian hater, Mister Cutler. I've had my reasons for not liking particular In'ians such as old Plume, but yes indeed, I've known some I liked. In fact when I was a girl I knew quite a few I liked, and that liked me."

Sam returned with wide eyes and dropped down to open a sweaty hand. He said, "Look," and shoved the open hand under Frank's nose. "It was lying on the surface of the ground a little ways up the creek."

Frank looked, picked up one of the little rocks, and looked closer. He started to speak, then offered Skye the stone which she took, scratched, examined briefly, and handed back to Sam. "Pyrite," she said.

Sam's gaze wavered. "Gold?"

"No Sam, it's iron pyrite. What folks call fool's gold. It looks like gold, but it's worthless." She smiled at his crestfallen look. "But there is gold around. It's not lying atop the ground, but it's around. My father used to take a couple of horses and go prospecting every summer for a few weeks. He had bottles of gold. I still have them. . . . If you'd like, Sam, when we have slack time at the ranch, you can come up here and pan."

Frank arose, dusted off, and went after the horses. When he returned leading them, Skye was showing Sam how to test the weight of gold. She was holding a small nugget from a necklace Frank had not seen around her neck. They were kneeling side by side at the creek. Each time Skye dropped the nugget, it sank immediately to the bottom of the water. The pyrite Sam had found sank more slowly.

Sam was impressed. He tried it several

times, then handed back her nugget and looked at her. Frank turned away to grin. He had once had a similar experience, and knew what Sam was thinking: How could a woman be that savvy?

She led them west along the near side of the creek while more birds rose up in panic. They rode a full mile in the shade of willows before she found the gravelly ford she had been seeking, then they splashed across and rode directly toward the dark, unfriendly looking uplands. By then the sun was gone, but the vast grasslands southward were still bathed in early summer light, although where they were heading it was already dark.

CHAPTER 10

Horses

Skye Cameron knew the mountains; even with diminished visibility she sashayed among the huge old trees and brought them to a good game trail. Without a word she led them to a sump-spring meadow of about twenty acres with good grass and an almost completely delapidated log lean-to. While they were unsaddling she told them her father had built the lean-to, and that was all she told them about it until the horses were hobbled out a short distance and they had gathered firewood. Then she tossed aside her bedroll and said, "He brought me up here when I was old enough to make the ride, and we hunted, prospected a little, and made jerky. He loved the mountains. He grew up in the mountains of Tennessee."

She would have prepared their meal but

Frank eased her aside, and when she stared at him, he stared straight back.

She went over and dug out a pony of rye whiskey from one saddlebag and returned to their fire with it. Frank and Sam each had a drink, then she put it aside without drinking herself. She tossed her hat nearby, shook out her hair, and smiled at Sam. "I'm glad you're willing to give me a chance," she told him. Sam got red in the face but neither she nor Frank could make that out in the forest gloom.

They ate in almost complete silence. Later, when Sam walked out to the horses, Frank lit a smoke and gazed steadily across the fire. They'd had their first face-down at the stone ring about who would make supper. She had yielded. She was a very handsome woman. In fact, in all the ways that mattered to him, she was more of a woman than any Frank had ever known. But Sam had been right about one thing: she was domineering. He inhaled, exhaled, and smiled across the dying flames. She smiled back and remained silent. He said, "Miss Cameron, it would take a little time for a man to get used to someone like you."

"Why, Mister Cutler?"

He struggled with that, and nearly came up tongue-tied. "Well, it's hard to say."

"Shall I help you, Mister Cutler? Because I'm the boss."

He nodded slightly. "Partly, I reckon that's it. Partly it's because you don't ever let us forget it."

She lowered her gaze to the little fire ring. "Frank, in Cameron ranch there are thousands of acres, thousands of cattle, seven men, undependable weather, unpredictable troubles — like this one — and only me to make sure the bad things don't overwhelm me and the ranch." Her eyes swept back to his face. "You're a grown man; you've known sweet, charming women. How would they handle things if their father died leaving them something like Cameron ranch?"

He laughed at the directness of her look and manner. Instead of answering the question, he said, "I understand."

". . . But?"

He inwardly squirmed and ended up smiling at her. "It sure is a beautiful night, isn't it, ma'am?"

But she was not ready to let it pass. She did not return his smile. "Don't call me ma'am. Call me Skye."

"Yes'm . . . Skye."

"Don't laugh at me, Frank."

He slowly shook his head, meeting her gaze

head-on without speaking.

"Do you know what I'd like above everything else?"

He continued to gaze at her without speaking.

She dropped her eyes to the dying little flames again. "Someone to talk to."

He dropped his smoke into the fire. "Would I do?"

She looked up again. "I don't know. Would you?"

"Care to try, ma'am . . . Skye?"

"Have you ever been married, Frank?"

"No."

"Do you have any family?"

"No. I was an orphan."

"Then you know what loneliness is. What you know of it, triple it and you'll have an idea what life is for me."

He had listened long enough. "Where I spent quite a few years, Skye, they figure the number of cattle they can run per section of land roughly accordin' to the number of inches of rain they get per year."

She was staring at him.

He smiled. "I think you'll die on Cameron ranch, Skye. I don't think you'd ever be happy anywhere else. . . . What I'm aiming at is — in the first place you don't have to be

117

lonely. I have an idea you didn't originally figure to be but now you are, and you don't like it, but you won't do a damned thing about it because you've decided to be nothin' but the ranch boss."

She continued to stare at him. After a long time she stood up and walked out into the night. Frank watched her go and did not regret what he had said because he did not really believe she wanted someone to talk to as much as she wanted someone just to listen to her. And that would have been agreeable to him, he had always been a good listener, except that with Skye Cameron for some damned fool reason he did not want to just listen, he wanted to yank some of the slack out of her. He'd learned long ago that inward people were irrational people.

He was still sitting alone by the embers of their fire when Sam returned, looked around for Skye but did not mention her, and unrolled his blankets. As he sat down to kick off his boots he said, "Tell me straight out, Frank. Do you think we'll find those sons of bitches?"

"You can find anyone, Sam, if you're willing to keep at it long enough."

Sam was curling his gun belt when he replied to that. "That's about like something my pa would have said."

Frank sat there gazing at Sam Morton; how was it that other folks, in this instance Skye Cameron, could see things happening that he hadn't been able to see? He arose to walk out among the trees, Sam rolled in, the fire continued to burn down, and when Frank eventually returned, Skye was also bedded down slightly apart and with her back to him.

Very late something awakened Frank. He did not move. It was a rough, careless sound. He rolled over, reached for his gun, and sat up. The sound came again, closer. Frank faced toward it and shouted. "Get away from here you old bastard." For a long time there was utter stillness, then the sound returned as a large animal went shambling off in a different direction. Sam asked, "What was it, Frank?"

"A damned bear. Go back to sleep."

In the cold and eerie forest dawn Skye scrubbed at the spring and was making a fire when Sam and Frank rolled out to also head for the spring. When they returned she had coffee boiling and jerky stew heating. Without looking up she said, "When it is light enough we'll have to quarter for their tracks."

Frank sank down across from her and said, "Good morning."

She still refused to look up. "Good morning."

Sam filled a tin cup and blew on the coffee. He, at least, had no inward troubles bothering him.

When they struck camp Skye led them eastward on a good game trail, then began an angling climb around the haunch of their mountain. The horses were walking over spongy layers of pine and fir needles which muffled every sound. The air smelled of running sap; cold or not, it was still the time of year for that.

The columbines were out, shy and fragile, grass grew where it dared, usually nowhere near the huge trees, and once a large, bitterly protesting jaybird sprang from treetop to treetop denouncing their intrusion until they passed out of his territory. Skye rode bundled in her coat without looking around or speaking until they intersected another trail, where she stopped and sat like a carving for a long time, then pointed with one gloved hand.

"There you are. Two shod, one barefoot."

Frank looked from the tracks up the slope where the new trail went. "What's up there?"

"Two glades. The first one is smallest, about a mile along, the larger glade is about three miles up and it has some caves in the rock bluff which forms its north border."

"Broncos?"

She did not look at him. "No. Their rancherias are mostly east of here and much higher, up beneath the rims."

Sam edged around them to look at the tracks. "How old do you figure those tracks are?" he asked, and she answered shortly. "Yesterday."

Frank shifted in the saddle. If she was correct, then those horse-stealing sons of bitches had indeed loafed in camp. He could understand them doing that; aside from being miles west of where they had done their raiding, or whatever it was they had done, they were now safe in a forest where no one could see them.

Skye finally faced Frank. "Do you want to take the lead?" she asked. For a long moment they exchanged stares, then he nodded.

The new trail did not follow out around the slope as most game trails did, and that made it hard going for the horses. Frank consoled himself with the thought that if the outlaws had used it, with one worn-out horse to slow them down, they had probably not made their night camp very far ahead. And following out this line of thought, he also speculated that since they had loafed in their previous camp and probably felt quite safe, they may have loafed in the last night's camp as well.

That would make a difference. It would also make danger closer, so he stopped occasionally to look and listen.

They rode to the verge of the first meadow and sat their horses looking out where sunlight shone. There was no sign of three horses, three men, or a place where anyone had camped. As Frank turned back Skye said, "It will be the upper park then."

He nodded, looking across at her. "Would you like me to apologize, ma'am?"

She did not return his gaze. "Do you think that is necessary?"

He answered in one word. "No."

"You meant it?"

"Every word of it."

She hauled back to take her place behind his horse on the trail, and Sam, who had heard the exchange without understanding any of it, looked in wonder from one of them to the other.

Heat came a little at a time, and it never reached the degree of the heat back on the open range, but they shed their coats and lashed them atop the bedrolls behind their cantles.

Skye's estimate of three miles to the large glade turned out, in Frank's mind anyway, to be closer to five miles. He had his first sighting through some mammoth fir trees on his left, and he turned off the trail, working through the timber until he reached the last stand before the meadow began. They all dismounted; their horses needed the respite whether they found anything out there or not.

Frank held Sam's reins while the younger man went in and out among the trees to scout southward where the meadow curved offering a fuller view of its northern reaches.

Skye finished studying the meadow and turned. "Frank, you were wrong about the old In'ian and some other things."

He did not need to be reminded. "Yes'm."

"You said you were wrong about me too."

"Yes'm."

Her eyes seemed to darken with a degree of wry humor. "Well, wouldn't you think you would be entitled to be right once?"

He looked down into her face. "Go on."

Her color mounted. "What do you mean — go on? Do you have to be hit over the head with a log to know what wood is?"

He drew in a deep breath and exhaled slowly. He thought he knew what was in her mind but had no intention of putting it into words, because if he were wrong again, it would be very embarrassing.

She kept looking at him, and finally, when she realized he was not going to speak, she said, "Last night . . . I think you were right. It made me mad when you said it, and I lay awake last night still mad — and humiliated I guess — because I was afraid you were right. . . . That's what I mean. You're entitled to be right once in a while."

Sam returned with quick, springy steps. "Frank . . . they're out there in the grass up near a big wall of black rock."

"All three of them?"

"Yeah. Your *grulla*, my horse, and another one, a sorrel."

Frank gestured for Sam to lead the way down where he had been when he had seen their animals. It was a fair distance. When they cleared a flourishing, large thicket of some kind of thorny underbrush, Frank had a perfect view of the entire meadow. It was not only large in three directions, but that nearly perpendicular wall of rough black rock at the north end did indeed have caves along its base, and from one of them a man emerged to stand in brilliant sunshine and look toward the horses. He was too distant for any kind of detail to stand out, but Frank thought he was bearded. The man turned to his right and went along the base of the cliff and passed from sight where some pale-barked aspen trees grew in a clump, dwarfed by the mighty fir trees around them.

Frank plunged both hands into his trouser pockets and stood a long time without moving or making a sound. When his reverie was finished he said, "We'd better go back and hide the horses."

That was all he said until they had gone back, taken the animals deeper into the easterly forest, and left them hidden over there. He and Sam pulled loose their saddle guns. Skye did the same and turned to find both men gazing at her.

She said, "Don't be ridiculous, Frank."

His response was equally as short. "You stay here."

"I will not."

"Skye, I'm not asking you, I'm telling you. You stay here with the horses." He saw the anger coming and raised a hand. "That's it. I'll throw you and tie you like a calf, or you can do as I said without that." He lowered his hand. "Skye . . . ?"

She could have read the concern in his gaze from twice as far away. "Be careful, Frank. Be careful, both of you."

They walked away leaving her gripping the carbine as though she meant to crush it.

CHAPTER 11

An Ambush

Frank was unhurried in his reapproach to the meadow, and he moved ahead on an uphill tangent, so that when they were pressing close to the timbered verge again, they were much closer to the basalt cliff.

Sam stopped when the older man did and fished around for his chewing plug. He leaned the Winchester aside, got his cud settled, spat once, then said, "There's no one in sight now; how do we get 'em to come out?"

Frank was eyeing his *grulla* horse and did not answer for a moment. The horse was sweat-streaked and tucked-up. Whoever had been on it had been merciless, and that made Frank's blood boil because the *grulla* was as honest and trusting as the day was long. Abusing that kind of a horse was about like kicking a puppy or a little kid.

The horses were not very far from where he and Sam were standing in forest shadow. Frank finally replied to Sam while turning his attention northward, to the large, dark holes in the black-rock high barranca. "Getting them out doesn't worry me as much as what'll happen when they come out. . . . How long do you expect it would take you to skirt around that bluff and get atop it?"

Sam eyed the cliff for a long time before replying. "I've got an idea. Depends on what I run into on the way up there. . . . Maybe a half hour, maybe longer if it's hard climbing. Why?"

"Because we've got the drop and I'd like to keep it, Sam. I know you're heroic and all, because you told me you were, but I'm not." Frank turned and met Sam's gaze. "If you're atop that bluff and I run off the horses, they're going to come out. When they come out, they're going to be wild as scorpions. With you in back of them on the bluff, and me down here in front of them, we ought to be able to end this quick."

Sam said, "For me that'd be shooting them in the back, Frank."

For a while there was silence while Frank turned back to studying the cliff and the caves along its base. Then he said, "It might at that. . . . Remember what I told you about havin' just one instinct? We're going to survive, Sam; sons of bitches like those fellers aren't. They made the rules, we didn't. . . . They'd shoot you in the back in a minute. It's their game and their rules." Frank turned. "All right, you stay here and I'll climb up there. . . . One other thing, Sam, you're young. Your future lies ahead of you. No damned renegade outlaw on earth is worth you getting killed over."

Sam lifted the Winchester and bobbed his head; then he turned up through the trees with a springy and purposeful step. Frank watched him go out of sight, then loosened his coat, leaned his carbine against a tree, and slowly knelt to pick up a half a dozen round stones.

Two men emerged from the cave with the largest and highest opening. They went only as far as a punky old deadfall of pine and sat there in midday warmth. They had a bottle which they passed back and forth. Eventually, another man came over to the deadfall and they handed him the bottle, but he refused it and rolled a smoke. He was a large man with bushy hair and thick black sideburns.

The large man lit up, exhaled, and gestured

as he spoke. Frank could hear the voice but could not distinguish what was being said. He was within carbine range, and those unsuspecting outlaws wore only side arms.

One man laughed coarsely. His companion on the log turned suddenly as though listening, then spoke, and the other two also faced eastward. Frank held his breath. Sam was evidently moving past the cliff face and had stepped on a twig or had perhaps loosened some rocks.

The large man grunted and said something curt. His companions faced forward again and one of them reached for the bottle.

There were wild animals up in here; some, like wapiti, were nearly as large as horses, and others, by the dozens, were much smaller and very numerous. In similar circumstances Frank would also have attributed any slight sound to them.

The horses grazed closer and Frank alternately eyed them and the loafing men soaking up sunlight warmth. Conditions were ideal at this moment; perhaps in another fifteen minutes or so they would not be. He tried to see up along the top of the barranca, but there was too much underbrush among the trees; a whole platoon of men could have been moving up there and he would not have been able to detect their presence.

One of the outlaws returned to the big cave, and moments later emerged with two dented cooking pans. He headed for a stone cooking ring and his companions watched for a while, then one of them called over. Frank heard every word this time.

"Anybody that eats as often as you, has worms."

The kneeling man whittling shavings for his fire did not answer. He was busy. The other two turned their backs on him, sat in pleasant warmth on the old deadfall, and gazed down where the horses were grazing. Frank did not move so much as a finger.

Then the horses finally began grazing away, westerly, and Frank squinted hard all along the cliff top. If the horses moved out of a stone's throw, he would be in trouble.

A momentary, two-second flash of sunlight off gray metal directly above the caves caught Frank's attention. Sam was squirming into place. Frank looked at the horses and at the outlaws, then very slowly sank to one knee and cradled the saddle gun in the bend of his left arm as he hauled back to throw the first stone. It fell short, but it made one of the horses turn and stare.

He threw another stone, and this time his

aim was nearly perfect. He even heard the solid sound as the rock bounced off a horse's rib cage. That time the reaction was different. He was aiming to throw again as the startled horse flinched, spun with his hobbled forelegs in the air, and came down hopping.

The next stone hit him on the rump. He needed no additional inducement to hop as fast as he could. Frank flung his last two stones and hit his *grulla*, who was already beginning to spook. The *grulla* could hop faster than a man could run; he'd had years of experience with hobbles. He passed the other frightened animal with a loud snort, and all three horses turned southward fleeing as fast as hobbles permitted.

The man at the fire ring jumped up and yelled. His friends sprang off the log and stared. One of them abruptly ran toward the cave. When he rushed forth again, he had two carbines, one of which he tossed to the man at the stone ring. Then all three of them started down the meadow after the horses.

Frank was still down on one knee. He methodically raised his left hand, braced it against a rough-barked fir tree, eased the Winchester across the braced forearm, and waited.

The outlaws were too far now to retreat in haste to their cave. They were perfect targets.

Frank's finger curled inside his trigger guard as he tracked the lead runner, the large man with the black sideburns. He pulled in a deep breath and called out.

"Hold it! Right where you are!"

They reacted about as Frank had expected them to. For one fleeting moment they were so astonished that all they did was turn their faces toward the sound of that voice. Then they dropped flat and fired. They continued to fire. One of them had no saddle gun and his Colt made a much louder and deeper roar than the Winchesters of his companions, but it was nowhere nearly as accurate at that distance.

Frank heard only one of those searching bullets; it struck a rock which exploded into fragments. Frank squeezed off a shot, and the big man sprang off the ground and began to frantically roll.

From atop the cliff Sam fired twice, very fast. Frank saw the outlaws react to this with panicky consternation. He waited until the large man stopped rolling and raised up staring northward, and then shot him through the head. The large man flopped and rolled.

The gunfire reached a deafening crescendo. The horses had gone southward; they had turned in terror and run directly toward the trees, leaving the meadow and disappearing into the forest.

Sam shifted slightly to track his next target. The man was coming down the barrel through Sam's buckhorn sights, when he fired twice again, very fast, and Frank's target jumped straight up, then dropped to his knees, hung there briefly like a gut-shot bear, then collapsed forward.

The third man ran blind. Having sprung to his feet, he ran in mindless terror toward the distant trees to the west. Frank tracked him through both gunsights and fired at about the same time Sam did again, twice very fast. Momentum plus the impact of bullets drove the running man ahead for about ten feet, with his legs tangling all the way. When he fell, his hat flew like a bird and landed still farther away.

Frank did not move for a long time. There was black powder gunsmoke out in the meadow where no wind moved it. It spread very slowly. Nothing was out there now but three dead man lying yards apart, and that greasy-looking smoke.

Nor was there any sound after the echoes chased one another to oblivion. Frank did not arise as he lowered his head and, using loose cartridges from a coat pocket, recharged the carbine. Then he leaned on it and waited.

He had not expected those men to yield, and he had not particularly cared about yelling for them to do so. They were not the first renegades he had encountered, but as far as he knew, they were the first ones who had made a fight out of it, at least in part because they had been swilling whiskey.

Eventually he arose when he heard someone coming through the trees. It was Sam Morton, his shirttail dragging, sweat soaking through the cloth in front, and his hat crushed down as though he might have lost it in the brush, had retrieved it, and had fiercely pulled it so low it could not leave him again.

He came on up and stared out into the sunlighted meadow without opening his mouth. Frank understood the look on the younger man's face; death was never attractive, but it was particularly unattractive when it had arrived as it had for those outlaws.

Staring out there did not do any good, so Frank said, "We better find the horses," and with the Winchester hanging from his fist, he turned and started southward. Sam followed.

There were punched away places in the fir needles where the horses had plunged away. They were easy to follow. They led eastward for a short distance, then swerved a little northward.

Frank came through the timber and saw six horses — the three wearing hobbles and the three he, Sam, and Skye had ridden up here — and Skye. She was facing the direction of whatever sounds Frank and Sam had been making, with her carbine in both hands, cocked and low. Her face was white to the hairline.

He walked on up, met her gaze briefly, stepped past to the side of the big, rawboned bay, upended his Winchester, and sank it into the saddle boot. Then he turned and said, "All three of them."

She eased down the hammer and grounded her saddle gun. "I heard you yell to them."

He eyed them both. They had every right to look shaken. "I'll take these three horses back and get the men tied onto them. I think we got enough daylight left to get back down to that first little meadow."

She said, "I'll help."

Frank shook his head. "You stay here. It won't be that much of a job anyway."

This time she did not argue, and when he took down his lariat Sam also took his rope down. They removed the hobbles and left her, walking stolidly back toward the meadow.

He did not go directly out there; he went northward to the barranca and left the timber to reach the big cave.

Inside, was a mound of saddlery, flung aside carelessly, and three saddlebags lying near some torn mail sacks farther back. The outlaws had been using letters and newspapers to kindle their cooking fires. Other articles from the plundered mail bags were scattered and trodden.

Without a word they saddled the horses. Then Frank returned to the cave to gather up most of the scattered mail and stow it inside two of the leather-reinforced, soiled mail pouches. When he came back out Sam held up something. It was three tidy bundles of greenbacks bound with fishline. "I guess they divvied it up. It was in the saddlebags along with some other personal stuff. . . . Sure as hell they stopped a stage or robbed a train."

Frank tied the pouches to a saddle. There had also been a Winchester leaning against some rocks in the cave, and three bedrolls as well as two gunnysacks of food. He did not go back after them.

He rolled and lit a cigarette and looked at Sam. "You can go back and stay with Skye, if you're of a mind to," he said.

Sam looked momentarily puzzled, then as

understanding came, he shook his head. "I've seen 'em before."

Frank smoked and surmised that Sam had never seen people the way these three looked, all shot to hell and wearing frozen expressions of raw horror. He dropped the smoke, ground it underfoot, reached for two sets of reins, and jerked his head. While they were walking southward, he said, "You did right proud. . . . I never heard a man use a carbine like that before. Shot twice so fast it almost sounded like one gunshot."

"My pa taught me. He said if you got to shoot at all, you want all the edge you can get. He showed me how to fire off the first round while beginnin' to lever up the next round."

The sun was moving in the direction of some peaks miles west of the basalt barranca. Its brilliance and heat were undiminished, and there were deerflies out upon the meadow, along with a faint, bitter scent of burnt gunpowder.

CHAPTER 12

Another Meadow

There was no way to make the dead men presentable, but Frank tried. He swaddled each man in blankets with his head covered. Even so, when the three of them were slanting back down the mountainside he told Skye to take the lead.

Silence seemed deepest as the light began to fade, and although none of them knew it, the sky which they only barely were able to see had been covered from horizon to horizon with that misty veil Frank had noticed before they had reached the timber. It was probably going to rain.

They had a sore-footed horse on their hands, so they had to travel slowly. The same horse was also not very strong. He trudged along with his head down, his dull eyes noticing very little.

When they finally turned off into the small meadow only a couple of miles above the foothills, Frank did not hobble the worn-out horse and took them all to water and scrubbed their backs. His *grulla* did not have a single white hair from sweat gall, and if Frank could prevent it, he never would have.

He remained out there with the horses for a while until Sam or Skye had a cooking fire lighted, but he stayed out there a while longer to work his way out of sight among some creek willows and peel down to bathe. The water was cold, and with daylight about gone, the air was not much warmer.

When he finally reached the camp they had set up, he felt much better. The corpses were lying side by side where he had placed them during the unsaddling an hour earlier. Skye and Sam had made camp so that everyone's back would be to them.

But they could talk, finally. Sam showed Frank some wilted greens in the cooking pot. "Wild onions," he announced. "She's even got some wild parsnips in the stew."

Frank grinned. "Mighty handy — for a woman, wouldn't you say, Sam?"

He caught the look he was getting from Skye without turning his head and laughed. Sam agreed. "For a fact she's handy."

Frank jerked his head. "There's a creek back yonder beyond the horses, Sam. We got no soap, but you can use dirt like the In'ians do."

At the younger man's expression, Frank shrugged. "You'll feel better. A man always does after he's washed off."

Sam walked out toward the horses and as soon as he was beyond hearing, Skye looked up. "That's how folks catch pneumonia, Frank."

"Don't worry, he won't do it. Wash a little is all. And it's a fact a man feels better after he's had an all-over scrubbing." He leaned to catch the aroma of her stew and coffee. It was better than the French toilet water he'd smelled on dance hall girls.

"Someday, you'll make a man a right fine wife, Skye. Not all women are cooks, but most think they are."

She leaned away from the fire and raised the back of one of her hands to push a heavy curl off her forehead. "If you think this is cooking, Frank, then you don't know one meal from another."

"I don't," he said in calm agreement. "I can remember once a long time ago eating a good meal. A Messican woman made it. Now that woman was a cook. . . . She was also a *curandera*."

Skye eyed him with doubt. "I know I shouldn't ask . . . what is a *curandera?*"

"Nothing bad. It's a healer. They use herbs and whatnot." His eyes twinkled at her. "Sometimes they use the guts out of chickens too. And they say some magic words."

"She did that to you?"

"Yes. I had . . . That's a waterless country on the southern end of Texas, and riding day in and day out, sweating a lot and all . . . hot saddle seat . . . "

"I'm willing to let it end there," she said, and bent over the little dry-wood fire which made blue flames without smoke. She changed the subject. "I think we should have buried them back up there, Frank."

"No. You can't make a decent grave using sticks and your fingers. We'll take them back down where we can get shovels and do it right. . . . Remember that bear the other night? They can open shallow graves in ten minutes."

She looked at him. "I've never been so frightened in my life."

"I wasn't exactly dancing a jig, myself."

"I don't mean the outlaws. I mean I was petrified that one of you would get shot, maybe killed."

He met her gaze unable to think of a single thing to say. Finally, because the silence was stretching out, he managed a comment. "They'd been drinking. Sam and I watched them up there passing a bottle around. Whiskey makes a man feel nine feet tall and bulletproof."

It did not change the expression on her face in the blue firelight. After a moment she returned to her cooking and had nothing more to say until he was rolling a smoke and she leaned, offering a lighted twig. "If they were mail robbers, there will likely be a reward on them."

He sat back and considered the glowing tip of his cigarette. "Maybe. I've never been in the reward business. All I wanted was to get my horse back. . . . You want to put in for the bounty?"

"I was thinking about Sam."

"Did you talk to him about it?"

"No . . . I was thinking it might help him amount to something."

Frank exhaled and looked steadily at her. "Maybe it would. Maybe he doesn't want to amount to something. Maybe he'd be happy hiring out as a rider. Lots of men are, Skye."

She bit her lip. "Don't twist things that I say, Frank. He's so young. By the time he's as old as . . ."

"As I am?"

She pulled back from the fire. "What's bothering you? You weren't so sensitive before."

He tossed the cigarette into the fire. "Excuse me. I guess I'm tired. . . . What were you going to say?"

She did not take it up again; instead she studied his face and eventually smiled at him, making such a bold announcement he was shocked. "I like you, Frank."

He was saved from having to reply by the arrival of Sam. He had scrubbed his face and hands, but as Frank had surmised, that was far as he had gone.

He sat down in silence and fidgeted a little. Then he held out a hand toward Skye. She leaned, looked at what was on his palm for a while, then picked it up, bit it, scratched it on one of the fire ring rocks, and finally said, "It's gold, Sam," and smiled at him. "You do better prospecting in the dark than in daylight."

Sam's expression changed. "Are you sure?"

"Yes. Where was it, at the creek?"

"Yeah. I was using sand to scrub off with. It was in the sand."

She handed back the tiny nugget. "You just made the first mistake a prospector can make. Never tell anyone where you made your strike.

My father used to say that if there was a permissible lie, it was to send people in the opposite direction from where you turned up color."

Sam showed his find to Frank. There were four nuggets, ranging in size from that of a pea to that of a wood tick. "We could set up camp here and maybe do better'n wages, Frank. I got a feelin' about that creek."

Frank laughed. "I've heard folks say there's no disease easier to catch than gold fever. . . . Maybe we'll do that." His blue gaze drifted slowly to Skye Cameron. "A man should better himself if he can. After all, he doesn't want to live out his life lookin' at the rear ends of cows."

She picked up a tin plate, slammed hot stew on it, and shoved it at Frank as though it were a dagger. He said "thanks" and did not look up until half his meal was gone.

Sam buried the nuggets in a trouser pocket and turned in shortly after he had eaten, to lie awake staring at the star-speckled, cobalt night.

Frank went out for a final look at the horses. Particularly at the dull-eyed, ridden-down, barefoot horse. The animal was still cropping grass after the *grulla* and the other animals had taken a hipshot stance while they dozed.

144

He turned to look northward, remembering every detail of those killings. There was a corner of his mind that would never sleep again.

A quiet voice said, "I'll loan Fred to you, if you want to build a cabin up here while you're prospecting."

He turned toward her.

"Fred is a good carpenter. In fact he's a better carpenter than he is a range man." She glanced over at the horses. "And no one will bother you."

That statement interested him. "Do you own this meadow?"

"Yes. All the way to that larger one." She stood looking at him. "Why did you make that remark to Sam about amounting to something?"

He cleared his throat.

"Somewhere, Frank, somehow, we've developed into antagonists. It wasn't like that at all before we reached the upper meadow. How did it happen?"

He was not aware of any particular antagonism. He did not really believe there was any, and he thought he knew what it was that had left her with that impression. "I got a bad habit, Skye. I tease people. I'm not antagonistic toward you. . . . In fact . . . I didn't mean to make you mad. But I got to admit it tickled me when I did. You puff up like a grouse and shoot sparks."

She stood motionless looking at him. All right, now that she knew, she also knew how to spoil his fun. She would not flare up at him. But she was also conscious of something else; she did not normally flare up when someone teased her. Then why did she do it when Frank teased her?

"Is there any coffee left?" he asked.

There was, about two cupfuls left. And, there was still some whiskey in the pony she'd brought with her. As they started back he looked down. "You said you liked me."

"Yes."

"Well, then I guess it's all right for me to say I like you, too."

Her shoulders moved. He looked closer but she stepped briskly ahead. She was not sure whether he would get angry, but because she preferred not to put it to the test, she did not want him to know she was struggling to keep from laughing. Frank Cutler had as many facets to him as a split rock, and he had just demonstrated one of them — he was as strong as oak and twice as thick.

Darkness hid the three dead men lying wrapped in blankets in a row, but Skye and

Frank sat by the dying little fire with their backs to them anyway as she filled two cups and handed him one. She tasted the coffee, which was hot but also bitter. He rolled a smoke, and she watched until it was lighted and then said, "You use too many of those things, Frank."

He put a calm glance upon her. "You are too bossy, Skye." He exhaled smoke then also said, "By golly, you're right, we are antagonistic to each other."

"I don't want to be right. And I shouldn't have said that."

He nodded in agreement. "That's a good start. Most folks would apologize, but you don't have to."

She could feel the heat rising inside and was unaware that her body had also stiffened, until she saw him gazing at her. She struggled. Then she let her breath out silently and smiled sweetly at him. "I apologize. . . . And you know what else?"

"No."

"If I were six feet tall an' weighed two hundred pounds I'd punch you right in the nose."

He blinked at her.

She held that sweet smile a moment longer before raising the dented tin cup in a salute to him. "I can't match you, Frank. I'm too tired." She put the cup aside. "In the morning could we start over?"

He sat there long after she had gone out into the darkness to her bedroll, solemnly watching the fire burn down to pink ash, and although it was his custom to have a final smoke before turning in, this night he did not roll one. Maybe he did use too many of the damned things.

CHAPTER 13

Southward from the Mountains

The sun was climbing by the time they rode away from the foothills out upon the open range. Sam watched Frank rub his bristly jaw and did the same. Then he said, "Sure be good to get a razor," and nodded slowly in agreement with himself.

Frank eyed Sam's almost invisible, downy face fuzz and with a grave expression agreed. "It sure will be. And a decent hot bath. And do some laundry at the creek. But most of all eat a big, stove-cooked meal."

Sam eyed Skye who was up ahead. "Then what?" At Frank's inquiring gaze, he also said, "Well, when we rode into her yard we were looking out for the old man. Now he's dead. Then we went after your horse. Now we got him back. What comes next?"

Frank had no opportunity to reply before

Skye reined back and twisted in the saddle. "Rider coming."

They halted, swung off, and waited beside their horses while the increasing heat of another new day warmed them. Skye finally said, "It's Fred."

Frank did not particularly care which of her riders it was; he was curious about anyone meeting them like this. He must have been waiting for them and watching.

While still a couple of hundred yards out, Fred dropped to a slogging walk, taking in the grisly sight. When he reached them and dismounted he nodded to the men and turned toward Skye. "There's a lawman with three fellers in the yard."

Skye accepted that with an unworried expression. "We have what they're looking for, Fred."

"No ma'am. They didn't know nothing about three outlaws crossing our range from the northeast." Fred paused. "They're lookin' for Frank and the lad."

Five seconds of absolute silence passed. Skye turned slowly and Frank ignored her gaze as he spoke to the lanky cowboy. "Where are they from?"

"The town of Powell some distance south of here." Fred was uncomfortable. He also was naturally curious as he gazed at the weathered, bewhiskered face of Frank Cutler. "They come in last night. We put them up. The lawman talked to Rand. That's about all I know, except that Rand come to me in the bunkhouse after dark and whispered for me to slip out, find you, and pass the warning."

Frank exhaled softly. Maybe the lawman would not attach significance to one missing range man, and maybe he would. There were no other visible horsemen in any direction.

Fred got off the subject. "Who was those fellers?" he asked, jutting his chin in the direction of the burdened horses, and when no one replied, he let it drop and pulled a pair of plaited rawhide reins through his gloved fingers, waiting.

Skye eventually said, "Frank . . . ?"

"We'll ride on in, Skye."

"That might not be the best thing to do, Frank."

All three of them were watching him. His lips lifted in a very faint smile. "Maybe not, but leaving you to take the horses on in without Sam and me doesn't strike me as the best thing either. Once you start running, you can't ever stop."

She was gazing steadily up into his face. She had a direct question framed on her lips but left it there unspoken as she turned and swung back across the saddle. She handed Fred the lead shanks, told Frank to do the same to Sam, and then said, "Ride ahead with me," and he obeyed.

When the little cavalcade was moving again, ant-sized in the sun-brightened miles of unrelieved grassland, she removed her gloves, stuffed them in a coat pocket, then also shed her coat and tied it behind. As she was turning she looked directly at the man beside her.

"I know what the custom is. I grew up knowing what it is. Never ask personal questions. But I have a right to know, haven't I?"

"Three mean freighters picked on Sam at the Powell saloon. He stood up to them. It would have been pure and simple murder. None of them was fast, but there were three of them, maybe fifteen feet away. They picked the quarrel. . . . I told Sam he'd been a fool to stand up to three armed bullies especially at that distance. . . . I took his side. . . . Afterwards we lit out and didn't stop for a while. He was grazed along the side. . . . He was almighty lucky they were slow."

"When you rode out, were they dead?"

"Yes'm."

"I have one question, Frank, and I want an honest answer."

He met her gaze head-on. "That's the only kind you'll ever get from me."

"Was it really a fair fight?"

He leaned, spat, straightened up, and twisted to look back where Fred and Sam were slouching along, not speaking. As he straightened forward he said, "According to the rules, Skye, it was a fair fight. They picked it, and they would have killed Sam. . . . They were bullies and they had been drinking, but their mistake was that they were not handy with guns."

She rode a hundred yards staring down-country where rooftops would shortly be visible. Then she said, "All right, the lawman will probably have warrants for you and Sam. . . . One lawman and three possemen don't match what I have, counting you and Sam. . . . " She looked around gravely. "Most likely the best we can do is run them off, and they'll be back in a few days with a bigger posse. . . . If you head due west you could be out of the territory in a couple of weeks. Out of any local lawman's jurisdiction."

He knew her well enough by now to discern even slight changes in the sound of her voice, and this change had not been altogether slight. It had been tinged with the same despair he had met with back up yonder when

153

they had first faced one another after the battle in the big meadow. He was thinking of how she looked now, and how she must feel, and for some little distance he rode quietly.

Eventually he said, "You'd be in trouble up to your gullet, and if they didn't scare away, someone would likely get hurt. . . . I'd like to thank you for the offer though, only I don't know exactly how to do it . . . do it right anyway . . . but we'll ride on in. It was a fair fight. There were witnesses. The barman for one."

She was skeptical. "Then why have they been hunting you?"

He shrugged. That question had occurred to him an hour earlier when Fred had first ridden up with the news. "I don't know. . . . We'll find out."

"Do you have friends in Powell, Frank?"

He shook his head. "No. I got in there during a bad storm and figured to stay only until it let up. I'd never seen the place before."

She rested both gloved hands atop the saddle horn. She was profiled to him with her jaw squarely set and her green eyes fixed upon the distant clutter of rooftops. Lynchings in cow country were part of a very old custom, going back to the days when there were no genuine law officers. Lynchings of strangers were ordinarily accomplished swiftly with full local approval.

There was a fee lawyer up at Fort McCall, a two-day trip from her yard. She knew where Powell was. Even if she could reach McCall in better than two days, and providing the lawyer was in town and available, they would then have about a four- or five-day stagecoach ride, ignoring the possibility of breakdowns, which were frequent, and they would probably not be able to get down to Powell in time to prevent a hanging.

Frank had spoken her name twice before she heard him and turned. He said, "Don't fret."

The green eyes were as hard as flint when she responded to that. "You are a damned fool, Frank."

He had heard women swear before over the years, but he had never gotten accustomed to it. He never would become accustomed to it, but he had never made an issue of it, and he did not do that now. "Skye, they got shots off. In fact before Sam was grazed a slug busted the front of the bar."

"You're not seeing clearly, Frank. I believe you. It was a fair fight. . . . Then why is a lawman with three deputies hunting you down?"

"We'll find out directly."

She yanked back to a halt, staring at him. "Once you're in the yard there are only two ways you'll be able to leave it — with them, or after my riders have run them off and you can head west with Sam."

"I told you we're not goin' to become fugitives. I know how that works. Even if it wouldn't bother me a hell of a lot, Sam's only nineteen." He met her gaze. "You think he ought to amount to something — how does he do that as a fugitive from the law for the rest of his life?"

She allowed her horse to move onward again. The animal knew where he was and by now he also knew where he was going. There was timothy hay and grain down there, and hot dust in the corral for him to roll in.

There was heat now from a yellow sun which was almost directly overhead. By now the men at the yard would have seen them approaching, and although they in turn could see the buildings distinctly, they were still too distant to see men.

She suddenly said, "Before I rode out to find you, I told Rand to bury the old In'ian."

He had not thought of old Plume lately. Nor did he know exactly what to say now. "Sam will like that. . . . I do too."

"Darned old devil," she muttered and said

no more for a long while until finally she looked back where Sam and Fred were plodding along, lead ropes around their saddle horns. Farther back the blanketed figures tied securely to saddles undulated gently with the movement of the animals under them. She straightened forward and spoke again, without taking her eyes off the nearing ranch structures.

"What am I supposed to do, Frank, sit home and twiddle my thumbs?"

He did not have an answer for that either. In fact it made him uncomfortable. "Well, I'll be back."

She gave her head a grating, short nod. "Sure you will. . . . I don't believe in ghosts. . . . Frank, I don't want you to go."

He reached to tip down the front of his hat. "I don't 'specially want to go."

"But you have to. . . . In my lifetime I've known two men I cared for. They were exactly like you, Frank . . . full of some notion of what a man must do — his duty. What the hell good will you be to me or anyone else when you're dead?"

He looked sharply at her. He was a patient individual but for the last few miles she had been getting increasingly distraught and even patient men had their limits. "Skye, I've told you — it was a fair fight. No one is going to get hanged. And there was something else; freighters down in Powell killed the town marshal not too long before Sam and I ran into this bunch. There won't be any crowd down there yelling to lynch us for killing some freighters."

"You know that for a fact, do you, Frank? You told me you'd never been in Powell before and knew no one down there. . . . People aren't rational after a killing. But if most of them were . . . It only takes three or four red-necks to yank on a hang-rope. . . . I'll bring along the riding crew and we'll go down there with you. . . . Don't get that look on your face, we're going along. Do you know for a fact this lawman and his possemen weren't friends of those dead men? Do you know for a fact that you and Sam will ever reach Powell alive?"

He gave it up and rode along gazing down-country in silence. When he was sure she had made her final statement, she suddenly said, "Frank . . . damn it, I can't let this happen to you. I just can't." She swung her head and rode most of the way to the yard looking west-erly, away from him.

Now, finally, it was possible to see men in the yard. The short one would be Carl, the taller man tugging at a droopy longhorn moustache would be Rand Belton. The four strangers were leaning silently on the barn hitchrack watching the riders approach, and back under the overhang of the bunkhouse was the unmistakable bulk of Homer the *cocinero* and another man whom Frank did not recognize because he was standing in shadows, but assumed he would be Mack, the range rider who was also a good tracker.

Those utterly still figures had probably been standing like that for a long time, very likely as interested in the blanketed corpses as they were in Frank and Sam, and perhaps Skye too.

One of the men straightened up in sunlight, and with one hand still resting atop the rack said something from the side of his mouth. The other three men also straightened up.

Frank had never seen any of them before. The obvious leader was a stalwart, graying man whose hair was too long and whose face was reddish bronze from exposure. His hat was dusty, and even in boots with drover's heels, he was taller than his companions.

The small metal circlet with the five-pointed star inside, was pinned prominently upon the front of his plaid flannel shirt. He did not move as the little cavalcade came down into the yard, but Rand and the other riders did. They went up to take the ropes from Sam and Fred and to lead the burdened horses into the barn to be unburdened and cared for.

Skye did not dismount for a few moments. She looked down at the graying man and said, "What do you want here?" It was not the ordinary greeting to strangers, but she had no intention of having this drag out.

The lawman looked straight back without changing expression or touching his hat brim to her. "My name is Bill Hanford, town marshal of Powell, south of here." Marshal Hanford removed his hat and drew two limp, folded papers from the sweatband. Without looking up again he replaced the hat and said, "I got two warrants, lady. One for that shaggy-headed gent beside you and one for that lad behind him." He stepped closer and held out the limp papers.

Skye had both hands atop her saddle horn and did not move either of them. "Warrants for what, Mister Hanford?"

"Murder," stated the stalwart, graying man, reddening a little as he stepped back with the papers in his hand. His stare at her was full of challenge. "Those two killed three men in the saloon at Powell. Unprovoked attack is the way it's written on these warrants."

Sam kneed his horse up beside Frank and said, "Unprovoked attack! Mister, that'a damned lie. They picked the fight and shot back." Sam raised one arm slightly. "You care to see where one of 'em hit me?"

The marshal looked coldly at Sam, then faced Frank without answering. "You'll be Frank Cutler?"

Behind the lawman, Rand, Mack, Carl, and Fred emerged from the barn and stood there, eyeing the marshal and his possemen. Frank dismounted and stepped forward to loop his reins before answering. He and the lawman had a couple of arm's lengths between them. "I'm Frank Cutler," he said, holding the marshal's gaze. "Who signed the complaints, Marshal?"

"I did, Mister Cutler. Then we took up the trail. You can't just ride into a town and murder people then head out and expect no one to come after you."

"You're right, Marshal, a man can't do that — if it's murder, which in this case it damned well wasn't, and there were witnesses."

Bill Hanford, who had already taken Frank Cutler's measure, shrugged a heavy shoulder. "All I'm required to do under the law is find 'em and bring 'em back. That's all. I get up a warrant and go find them. It's not my job to try them too. . . . Is that your blue horse?"

"It is."

"Well, since he's already saddled, suppose me and the deputies saddle up too, and we can start back before it gets dark."

Skye was dismounting when she said, "Our horses have had all they're going to stand for one day, Mister Hanford. . . . You can bed down in the bunkhouse for the night. . . . Supper will be ready directly." She held out her reins, Carl came over to take them and lead her horse away, and with all the men looking at her, she struck out for the main house. One of the possemen said, "She sure thinks she's the law, don't she?"

When he turned to assess the silence, there were six men staring directly at him with candid antagonism in each of their faces. He turned back and leaned down on the tie rack, studying the ground.

CHAPTER 14

Belton's Story

The four strangers were in a peculiar situation and were clearly aware of it. They ate supper at the cookhouse where even the cook was silently and obviously hostile to them. It was not a pleasant meal.

Too, aside from being on the Cameron ranch uninvited, they were outnumbered, and even though all four of them were capable-looking men, armed, rugged, and hard-bitten, if trouble came they would lose.

They stayed to themselves as dusk arrived and did not enter the bunkhouse until long after dark, when the lamp had been lighted and the nightly poker session was in progress.

None of the Cameron riders were impolite, they simply acted as though they were unaware the marshal and his possemen were among them.

Frank went out front to the porch and Rand Belton followed him. Rand said, "You could be so far from here come morning they'd never find you."

Frank had already been through this kind of a discussion once today and had no intention of enduring another one. He told Rand essentially the same thing he had told Skye Cameron: that it had been a fair fight, that there were witnesses, and that he was not afraid to return to Powell.

Rand had evidently had a meeting with his employer before supper because now he said, "It'll make quite a party, us, you, and them." He leaned against an upright. "We got enough work to do to last us until midsummer — and short-handed too." He sounded less resentful than irritated.

"Stay here and do it," Frank told him.

Rand snorted. "You don't know the boss. She said we'd all ride with you in the morning, except Homer."

Frank looked southward to the lighted main house. "Tell me something, Rand. That man she was supposed to marry — what was he like?"

Belton threw a sharp look of surprise at Cutler. "Who told you that story?"

Frank turned. "That's no answer."

"I never knew him. I hired on a short while after he disappeared. . . . The fellers who were here back then said he was a good stockman." Rand straightened up and went to a rickety chair, sat down, tilted the chair back, and said, "You know how long I been here? It don't matter, I guess, but I noticed something when you came riding in this afternoon. She was calling you by your first name and you was calling her Skye. In all the years I rode for her, I never once called her that. . . . She would have taken my head off."

Frank perched on the porch railing saying nothing. He did not like the idea of Skye and her crew riding down to Powell, and he could imagine the look on the town marshal's face when they all rigged up and rode out of the yard with him in the morning. He'd be red as a beet.

Rand suddenly said, "They said he was a good stockman. They all liked him. That's usually a pretty fair judgment, isn't it?"

Frank nodded. Rand was again on the topic of the man Skye Cameron probably would have married. He looked up and found the foreman's dark eyes fixed upon him. "Disappeared, went off somewhere lookin' for cattle, so they said, and never came back. Him, nor the horse."

Frank said, "In'ians?"

Rand's flinty eyes did not move. "No, it wasn't In'ians."

"You know that for a fact?"

"Yeah. For a damned fact. We used to have a horsebreaker on the place, feller named Pat Delahanty. From Missouri, I think he was. . . . We were troubled bad by wolves during the calving season about six years ago, so Pat and I loaded a packhorse with strychnine meat and went up into the mountains to get rid of the varmints. We made a dry camp one night — it was midsummer and there was light up until about nine o'clock. Not good light, but enough to make a camp by. Pat went down deep in a canyon hunting for water and came back with his face as white as a sheet."

Frank was motionless. "Dead man?"

"Yeah."

"Him?"

"Yeah. Everything was there with the bones: his horse shot through the head, his saddle and carbine, even his six-gun still tied into his holster, his spurs with his initials on the inside silver band, and his wallet. It had come out, I guess when someone pitched him down there, and fell under a big gray rock. Pat found it." Belton's eyes drifted away and did not return to Frank's face. "I ain't much

166

of a believer in things, Frank. He'd been there a long time, many years, and likely if Pat hadn't been thirsty he would never have been found. . . . just the metal stuff, his bones, and leather curled black and hard as a plank, except for that damned purse . . . I'll tell you what was in it. . . . You want to know?"

Frank rubbed his scratchy jaw. "Maybe not. Most likely it's your secret and you'd ought to keep it."

The range boss's dark, flinty eyes brightened in a peculiar way. "Two letters and some greenbacks. Nine dollars in greenbacks. . . . Them two letters was from his wife back in Nebraska."

Frank watched the wide, hard, and humorless smile spread across Belton's face. He had never cared for Rand Belton. They had gotten along, and once or twice the range boss had backed him because he had known that was what Skye Cameron had wanted him to do, but this was different. He could not imagine the reason for Belton telling him this story until Belton finally slammed down his chair and rose to enter the bunkhouse. Then he said, "I never told her or anyone else. . . . Pat quit and went down to New Messico to work. As far I know he's still down there. I'm goin' to go down and hunt him up directly. We was good friends."

Frank stood up. "It was best you didn't tell her," he said, and the range boss gently inclined his head. "You want to know how we knew it wasn't In'ians killed that feller? Because right after he rode out, the rest of the crew also rode out — and old Cameron rode out last. That much I got from Homer. But I never said anything to Homer. Pat and me found her pa's back brace down there too; busted in half; I guess when he picked that feller up after shooting him and flung him down there. . . . See you in the morning."

"Wait a minute, Rand. Why?"

Belton shrugged. "I can only guess. He seen one of those letters from that feller's wife back East. He was a hard, tough, cold-blooded old bastard. I've heard a lot of old-timers who knew him say that about him. . . . What would you have done if you found out some son of a bitch who had been sparkin' hell out of your daughter had an abandoned wife back East somewhere?"

The bunkhouse door closed softly after Belton, and Frank eased back down on the railing to methodically roll and light a smoke. He was still out there ten minutes later when all but one of the lights up at the main house went out; and after grinding out his smoke, he arose to stroll out back and look in on his *grulla* gelding, and to breathe deeply the pure, clean night air.

The sound of foot leather over loose dust brought him around. Skye said, "I thought you would be in bed." She looked scrubbed. Her blouse was pale blue and her riding trousers were immaculate, and again she was wearing those unmarred new boots. She came over to the corral and leaned looking in at the horses. "That gaunt one needs six months of rest and some good care, plus grain."

He continued to stand there looking at her. It seemed as though there was a scent of jasmine, almost indiscernible, coming from her hair.

She turned and looked up. "You haven't shaved. In the morning before we ride out, maybe Homer can cut your hair. He does it for the riders at two-bits a shearing." She smiled. "I couldn't sleep either."

He faced forward again, leaning in the star-bright warm night. "It's been quite a week," he said quietly, and turned at a very faint sound over behind the bunkhouse. She also turned. A hatless, stalwart man was standing over there with the red tip of a cigarette showing. Skye spoke in a murmur. "Marshal Hanford. I'm not surprised he'd want to know where you were, if you weren't in the bunkhouse. . . . Come along."

They strolled past the rear barn opening up as far as the ranch wagon shed, and there she stopped to say, "When I was a little girl my father brought me down here one day and showed me how to harness our driving horse."

"Did he go driving with you?"

"Once, but it was too painful. Just the first time; afterward he would come down here with me and help, then he'd stand here. When I was a half mile out I could still see him standing here."

"It must have hurt like the devil," Frank said, not looking at her.

"It did. Along toward the end of his life he began drinking more than usual."

"Did he ever go see a doctor?"

"Many times. Once he went all the way to Denver because someone told him there was a very good surgeon over there. . . . He came back and was in bed for three days."

"What did the surgeon say?"

She was leaning against the rough pine siding when she replied. "That he could remove the arrowpoint. The risk was about sixty-forty that if he did, Pa would never walk again.

170

He had his laudanum and later on his laudanum and whiskey. He told me he would not gamble on those odds when he'd been an active man all his life."

"Did he ever try to ride again, Skye?"

"Just once that I know of. He had Homer, who was a rider in those days, saddle a big sorrel he liked, and he took his carbine. He told Homer he just once more wanted to go hunting in the mountains. . . . When he returned we had to help him off the horse and into bed because his back brace had broken and he'd thrown it away. He never even tried to ride again."

Frank leaned on the siding, gazing in the direction of the shadowy, distant mountains, and when a faint sound reached him, he roused himself and stepped around the corner of the shed.

There was no glowing cigarette tip, but Hanford's silhouette was still down by the rear barn opening. Frank said, "Marshal, you better turn in. I'm not goin' to run out on you. You can have my word on it."

The silhouette did not respond, but after a while it turned and vanished wraithlike up through the barn.

Skye made a little grimace of dislike when he came back beside her. "I wouldn't trust that man as far as I could throw him."

Frank leaned in the mellow half-light and said, "I'm not much of a drinking man, but right now, tonight, I could use a drink."

She did not drink at all, but she responded easily. "I keep it at the house. For medicine." At his sidelong glance she exclaimed, "Really."

He walked with her the full distance to the main house, but from around behind the buildings on the west side of the yard, and shortly before they reached the porch, she cocked her head at him. "You don't believe me."

"About the whiskey? Sure I do. Anyway, it wouldn't matter. Lots of women have a drink."

"Yes. In dance halls and poker parlors. Is that where you saw them do it?"

He pulled off his hat as they entered. He watched her step to a handsome little marble-topped table and turn up the lamp wick. "I've seen some mighty respectable women take a drink now and then."

She pointed to a leather chair. "I'll be back in a minute."

He did not sit down but walked to the massive mantel over a great, black, fieldstone fireplace and gazed a long time at a handsome woman in sepia forever unsmiling behind glass inside a very ornate picture frame. She looked a little like Skye.

Then he looked a longer length of time at the hard-faced man in his middle years in an adjoining frame of the identical design. Here, the similarity was more marked. The man looking directly back at Frank had heavy cheekbones, a strong, unyielding, wide, thin mouth, and a neck which was almost too columnar for the collar enclosing it. The eyes told their story of a man who had matured in hardship and danger, a bad man for an enemy, and not an individual who would forgive anything he considered a violation of his private code.

"Those are my parents," Skye said, approaching with his watered whiskey.

He smiled at her. "There's a little of you in both their faces."

She went to a chair and sat down opposite him with lamplight lying between them. With clasped hands and in this setting she did not seem to be the same woman who had been up in the big meadow with him. He smiled and sipped. The whiskey was good, and with its warmth spreading, he said, "I'm obliged . . . There are times when nothing can do for a man what one drink of whiskey can."

"The bottle's in the kitchen when you want more."

He had never been more than a one-jolt man, except upon rare occasions when he had become a two-jolt man. Tonight, if he had not been so dog-tired, he might have wanted a second drink.

She sat forward in the chair, watching him, and that got to be a little embarrassing. He looked at the ceiling trying to think of things to talk about, and had just about decided the weather would be a good topic, because it had not rained after all, when his glance drifted downward and stopped upon that hard-eyed man on the mantel with the heavy-boned face. And while they looked steadily at one another again, Frank forgot what it was he had meant to say.

A little later she accompanied him to the porch. Down across the yard there was the glow of a cigarette. He shook his head, thanked her, said good-night, and walked down off the porch on his way over to the bunkhouse.

She stood for a long time with the door latch in her hand behind her back. Even after Frank had entered the bunkhouse, she continued to stand there for a while.

CHAPTER 15

A Bad Time

They were all in front of the barn in the morning, and learned something about Marshal Hanford: the madder he got the calmer he acted and the softer his voice became.

He stood staring at Skye Cameron after she had told him she and her riders would accompany him and his prisoners down to Powell. Finally, he said, "If you're doing this because you figure Cutler and Morton need protection . . . they don't."

She turned slightly and said, "Saddle up," to the watching riders.

As they turned toward the barn Hanford also turned. "You don't come with us," he said in a very calm, soft tone of voice.

They stopped and swung to face Hanford and his three possemen. Counting Frank and Sam, there were six of them, all armed, all staring blankly at the lawman. The range boss said, "Mister, we don't work for you, we work for her." Then they lingered until Hanford turned his back on them to face their employer again, and they all went into the barn for their catch-ropes before heading out back for horses.

Marshal Hanford's three possemen waited a moment or two, then also went after horses. When they were alone at the tie rack, Skye said, "Why should you object, Marshal?"

"Because we don't need no escort, ma'am."

She held his gaze. "But maybe Frank and Sam do."

His pale eyes bored into her. "Mind explaining that, ma'am?"

She turned and walked toward the barn. Inside, Carl was rigging out a horse for her and held forth the reins which she took. Homer came wheezing across the yard with three laden army saddlebags and draped them over the hitch pole. He smiled uncertainly at Skye. "Enough grub to get you most of the way, I hope, ma'am." He could see the men saddling up inside the barn and looked a little wistful. Skye led her horse out, smiled at Homer, and said, "Thank you. Mind things. Jim ought to be back from Fort McCall today or tomorrow. He and the blacksmith — if the blacksmith comes back. You'll have company."

They left the yard on an angling southeasterly course, and Hanford's possemen managed to be in the rear while the marshal rode up ahead by himself, sitting his saddle with a very erect bearing. He was still furious.

Sam and Frank rode stirrup. When they were a mile out Sam said, "How come he didn't disarm us, Frank?"

Carl, the sloping-shouldered short man was directly behind Sam and offered his opinion before Frank could answer. "I'd guess because he didn't want to try it."

The sun arrived but no warmth came into the morning until they were a fair distance down-country. When they halted to water the stock at a creek, everyone shed their coats. When they left the creek still heading southeasterly, Rand Belton and Skye rode side by side, talking.

Carl had Fred Hudson on his right, but he acted as though he were alone. His expression was always testy, but this morning it was more so. When Fred offered a plug, Carl accepted, gnawed off a cud, handed it back, and grunted his thanks. He spat, wagged his head, and turned toward Fred. "This is a hell of a waste of time, us goin' all the way down to Powell when we got work pilin' up at home. . . . Frank's an idiot. If I'd been in his boots I'd be thirty miles west by now, where that son of a bitch up yonder couldn't ever catch up."

Fred had nothing to say. By nature he was much less forceful in his thoughts, and actions, than Carl. Another mile along he said, "Someone should have stayed back to bury them dead outlaws."

That thought did not trouble Carl. "Maybe Jim'll get back today or tomorrow. Him and Homer can do it."

"Jim's got a busted arm, Carl."

"Then let 'em lie under their blankets in the barn for all I care," exclaimed Carl.

When they halted at high noon near a bosque of white oaks, Skye came back where Frank was hobbling the *grulla*. "Rand told me he is going to quit after the gather is made when we get back," she said.

Frank was on his knees in the grass beside his horse and neither looked up nor spoke until he had finished with the hobbling. During that interval he thought of what the range boss had told him last night on the bunkhouse porch.

He stood up and dusted both knees. "I guess he figures he has to, Skye."

"Why?"

He met her mildly perplexed green gaze and shrugged. "You know how range men are as well as I do. . . . They drift. Even the ones with good jobs who've been with one outfit a long time."

"I think it's more than that," she told him and waited, but he had nothing more to say on this subject. Last night he had guessed what was in the foreman's mind. It had not set well with Rand Belton that she and Frank had been addressing one another by their first names. Maybe he had noticed other things as well; Belton was an observant individual and he was no fool.

When she clearly was not going to move until he spoke, he finally said, "Well, it's his decision."

"I'll tell you exactly what he said. 'You don't need me any more. You got another man who can do the job.' Then he rode over where Mack was."

His roaming gaze saw Rand and Mack eating with Carl, Sam, and Fred, sitting in the grass slightly apart from the possemen. They were eating in silence, but Hanford and his three companions were muttering among themselves as they ate. Mostly, they appeared to be listening to the marshal, and whatever he was telling them seemed to be having an effect. They sat there listening, eating slowly, and looking solemn.

Skye watched Frank's face. He glanced back, saw her doing this, and smiled. "It's not that hard to find a range boss. I wouldn't worry about it."

When the men were ready to ride again and arose to dust off, she turned toward her horse as Marshal Hanford walked toward Frank and said, "I'll take care of your gun for you." Everyone heard and turned to watch. The possemen were obviously not surprised and were standing slightly apart from one another as they watched.

Frank said, "You waited long enough," and the lawman's face reddened at this obvious allusion to the fact that Hanford had been afraid to try this back in the ranch yard.

He held out his left hand for the gun, and Frank lifted it out and passed it over. Hanford shoved the gun into his waistband and turned on his heel. He went over to confront Sam, who was standing on the left side of his horse near Mack, Rand, and Fred. "Yours too," he said in a more confident tone of voice.

Carl's face darkened. He was having a struggle of it to keep silent. Sam looked past Hanford, and Frank nodded his head slightly. Sam lifted out the old gun with the yellowing ivory handles and did not meet the lawman's gaze as he held it out. Hanford turned with the gun hanging at his side and said, "From here on Cutler and Morton will ride in back with me and my deputies."

That was too much for Carl. "Like hell," he said evenly. "You're still on Cameron range, mister, an' I don't give a damn whether you got a badge or not, you don't give orders."

Carl was ready to fight. Mack too was looking steadily at the marshal. Fred, a little pale but resolute, already had his gloveless right hand resting upon the upthrust handle of his holstered Colt.

Hanford gazed steadily at the shorter man. "Mister, you start something and you'll regret it. We're ready." He rolled his head slightly to one side to indicate the position of his possemen.

Skye Cameron was two yards behind Marshal Hanford beside her horse when she spoke. "Turn around, Marshal."

He obeyed and she cocked the gun in her hand. She did not say a word, simply cocked the gun and looked into Hanford's face.

Except for some birds in the oaks there was not a sound until Marshal Hanford shrugged and said, "Lady, we got a long way to go. You got a long way to change your mind about interfering with a law officer in the performance of his duty."

She tipped down the gun barrel from his chest to his belt. "Drop those guns on the ground, Marshal. I'll take care of them."

His face was a study in leashed fury. "I'm not going to toss these weapons down, an' if you pull that trigger there's going to be a massacre here, an' you bein' a woman isn't going to make one damned bit of difference."

Frank was too distant, but Sam wasn't. He started forward. He covered more than half the distance before one of the possemen called out.

"Hold it! Hold it right where you are, cowboy!"

Carl turned on the possemen with a snarl. Fred and Mack also faced around. For the five or six seconds the uncertainty lingered, Sam reached the marshal and with an upraised hand bent into a claw, turned him. They were less than two feet apart. Sam said, "Drop my gun," and when Hanford instead tightened his grip on it, Sam's right arm blurred upward and inward. The sound of bone over bone was like stones striking. Hanford went backward, dropped the gun, and raised a futile guard. His head was ringing, his eyes were not focusing, and his legs were wobbly.

Sam picked up his six-gun and stood facing the marshal with the gun in his right hand. Mack suddenly said, "Finish it, Sam."

Frank spoke sharply. "That's enough! Sam, give him back the gun!"

Even the possemen were staring.

"Shuck out the loads and hand it back to him, Sam."

The younger man looked a long time at Frank, then without a word, flipped opened the gate, shucked out the loads, and tossed his gun down at Marshal Hanford's feet. Then he turned his back on Frank and went over beside his horse.

Frank's initiative lasted long enough for him to give the lawman an order. "Get mounted up, Marshal. You and your deputies ride out in front and stay up there."

One posseman helped Hanford up astride, then he and his companions also mounted. They waited until the Cameron riders were also astride, then turned and woodenly rode out ahead.

Mack's fierce mood did not pass. He and Sam rode up beside Frank, and Carl's voice rang with deep disgust. "What the hell's wrong with you?"

Frank answered shortly. "He was right; it would have been a massacre, and that includes Skye. . . . For what?"

But Carl's anger did not diminish as he rode up where Fred and Mack were slouching along, to join them. Sam remained with Frank and was bitterly silent until they were farther along with the sun crossing above, then he blew out a big breath and looked over with a twisted smile.

Frank smiled back. "I told you last month, partner, there's a time to backwater and a time not to."

Sam gazed up ahead where the possemen were riding all in a bunch. "Yeah, I know. But that gun belonged to my pa." He dug out a lint-encrusted plug and offered it to Frank, who wryly declined, so he bit off a chew by himself.

Skye came back to join them. Frank eyed her thoughtfully. He had not noticed a gun belt. "Where did you carry that thing?"

"Inside my shirt, in back." She looked past him to Sam. "Your pistol's in my saddlebag. I'll take care of it."

For a while nothing more was said. There had never been anything but tolerance between the Cameron riders and the possemen, but now that had been stretched to the limit.

Frank watched Hanford up ahead. He had recovered from being struck before the cavalcade had covered two miles, but he was not a man who would forget, or forgive, being beaten, particularly in front of his own riders — and a woman. This was not over yet.

Frank looked for Carl and found him. He and the range boss were making conversation. It was not difficult to imagine what they might be talking about — that fool back yonder with their boss and the recalcitrant younger man.

Maybe they had been correct; maybe Frank and Sam should have cut and run for it last night. If they had, none of this would have happened today, and whatever lay ahead before they reached Powell would not happen either.

Hindsight, an old man had once told Frank Cutler, was a hell of a lot better than foresight.

They did not halt again until late afternoon when they came to one of the springs Frank and Sam had camped by on their flight northward. The horses were allowed an hour to feed while the men sank down to smoke and studiously ignore one another.

Bill Hanford's covert gaze went to Sam several times as he lay in the grass smoking with his hat tipped forward. Frank was right, he would never allow what had happened to him back yonder to pass.

Skye came back from looking after her horse and sank down in the grass near Frank, saying, "The north-south stage road is east of us about ten miles. I think Hanford will head for it — if he knows the country. If he doesn't, he's going to have to face some timber and rocky hills up ahead, and the riding will be harder."

Frank nodded because he remembered this country from having crossed it heading northward before. He was sure Hanford had also come up through there on his manhunt, so he too would realize what was on ahead.

CHAPTER 16

Night Camp

Frank's speculation about Bill Hanford would be proved accurate. He and his riders began angling more easterly than southward. The others followed. As far as Frank was concerned it did not matter how they got down to Powell, but using the stage road would be easier because it had a gentler grade than the more direct and more rugged route had. If it prolonged the trip somewhat, it would at least be more favorable to their mounts.

Rand came up beside Frank to speak his mind about the night camp. He thought they should take turns staying awake, and when Frank looked at him, the range boss said, "I wouldn't put it past that son of a bitch to try and slit Sam's throat in the dark."

Frank did not share that suspicion, but since it would do no harm to have someone awake, he offered to take the first go-round. Rand was agreeable. In fact, as they rode along under the slanting sunrays, Rand became a little philosophical, and almost likable.

"Strange how things happen, sometimes," he said, eyeing the distant possemen. "You rode in taking up for an old In'ian and that looked like all there was to worry about. . . . Now look. Three dead outlaws back in the barn, those fellers up ahead takin' you down to be tried for murder — and us comin' along when it's none of our business."

Frank smiled. "You can go back, Rand."

The flinty eyes did not leave the backs of Hanford and his deputies. "Naw . . . I feel like Carl does. Anyway, I could use a trip to town."

For a while they rode in silence, then Frank said, "Why did you tell me that story last night about Skye's pa and the dead man you found?"

Rand's gaze shortened, went over where Skye and Sam were riding together, then drifted away.

Frank decided he was not going to get an answer so he spoke again. "You had to lay something on me, didn't you? You didn't like it that the boss and I were friendly, so you had to give me a handicap."

Rand offered no denial and he did not look at Frank either; he simply raised his left hand a little and as the horse started away, he said, "You take first watch, I'll take second. Mack and Fred can split what's left between them."

Frank looped his reins and rolled a cigarette. He had known for forty years that people were complicated and unpredictable. He lit up and looked at the position of the sun. Another couple of hours and they'd have to start watching for a place for the night. His gaze dropped to Rand Belton riding over with Carl. Unpredictable, and mostly with a varying streak of vindictiveness in them.

One of the possemen was pointing almost due eastward and talking to Marshal Hanford. Frank followed out the direction of the man's upraised arm and saw in the distance what appeared to be a pack outfit of perhaps ten animals and two or three riders.

Everyone saw the same thing, and while there had been little conversation up to now, after the sighting there was none at all as this fresh intrusion held everyone's attention.

Hanford and his men finally bunched up and talked. Wearing a quizzical expression, Skye rode over to Frank. As far as she knew there had been no pack outfits near her range since she had been a child. Nowadays there were roads that touched nearly all the settled places — not the isolated cow ranches like Cameron, but most of the places where people congregated in villages or towns.

Frank offered a suggestion. "Maybe they're traders bound for the reservation."

She scotched that notion. "Not any more. Anyone who wants to trade with the In'ians has to go directly to Fort McCall and get permission first."

He said, "Trappers?"

She frowned at him. "Not in summertime, Frank."

He said no more, although he did not feel this packtrain was all that unusual. He'd seen them all his life, one place or another.

The packers had evidently been watching them too. They changed course slightly to affect a juncture near some cottonwood trees. Beyond the trees it was possible to make out some cuts and burms where the north-south roadway was, still a couple of miles eastward.

When the packers got in among the old trees they swung off and began lifting down the *alforjas*. Frank smiled to himself. They were working fast; obviously there was water where the trees stood, and the packers meant to establish priority for a camping ground.

Hanford held up his left arm and stopped.

Everyone else also halted. One of the posse-men eased over into a lope, heading for the trees. Carl came over as Frank sat watching and said, "Puts me in mind of how things was when I was a kid."

Frank understood and nodded. He also remembered how men meeting in wide open country reconnoitered one another.

Carl spoke again. "That's a pretty big train. My guess is that they're heading west, a couple hunnert miles where there's a whole slew of mining camps in the mountains."

Frank nodded. He had not known there were mining camps to the west. He was watching the posseman as he swerved in among the cottonwoods and two men came forward on foot to meet him.

Carl said, "There's another place to camp, but it's on across the roadway and it'll be dark by the time we reach it. Over among them trees there's a warm-water spring." Evidently Carl knew this territory.

Frank turned toward the shorter man. "Big enough for all of us?"

Carl nodded. "Yeah. And fifty more."

Marshal Hanford was in earnest conversation with his remaining two possemen up ahead. Frank decided this might take a little time and swung to the ground. The other ranch riders saw this and emulated him. In storybooks men might sit on a horse's back when it was standing still for hours on end, but range men never did. A horse wasn't a chair.

Hanford's posseman did not return; he instead walked out away from the tree shade and wigwagged with his hat. Hanford started forward riding twisted in the saddle to make certain everyone followed. They all did.

There was a ripple of quiet speculation among the Cameron riders as they aimed for the trees. When they got closer Frank counted the pack animals: fifteen — and they were mules not horses.

The packers were back at work again, lifting off packsaddles — in this case McClellan saddles with T-irons screwed on in front and in back. The tree was longer; if a load was even, animals did not get tender or sore backs under a converted McClellan.

There were two, not three packers, which in part accounted for the vigorous way they worked. Fifteen mules and two saddle animals was about all two men wanted to handle in a train.

They were bearded men, unshorn, thick-shouldered, and friendly. They waved everyone on in, and when Skye walked her horse into tree shade, both packers eyed her with frank curiosity.

As everyone swung to the ground, the man who had scouted up the packers took Marshal Hanford to one side where they talked. Everyone else got busy unsaddling and making camp. Frank met Skye fetching water from the spring in a leaky, collapsible canvas bucket and took it from her. As they approached the Cameron ranch camp, she glanced around where one of the burly, bearded packers was smiling at her. She smiled back a little, then continued walking. The packer tossed down the britching he'd been holding and walked after them to the place where Sam and Fred were rummaging among the army saddlebags Homer had sent along. The freighter was probably nowhere nearly as old as he looked to be; lengthy exposure made it impossible to guess any range man's correct age. He had twinkling blue eyes and a wide smile. As he pulled off his hat he said, "Ma'am, I'm Jess Spooner. That feller yonder is my partner — Calvin Boggs. He's bashful. I ain't."

Skye told the freighter her name and in a slightly distant manner named Frank, Sam, and Fred. Then she said, "That's a large train, Mister Spooner," but he ignored her comment to say, "Sure never expected to see a lady way out here. It's a downright pleasure." He carelessly gestured. "We got trading goods and provisions. We're aiming for the placer camps westerly. It'll be another month before we see another lady."

Skye looked past Jess Spooner where his partner was glaring over his shoulder in Spooner's direction; there were still nine mules to be freed of their harness. Skye said, "I think your partner needs help, Mister Spooner."

He continued to smile admiringly at her. "He'll make out. Last week when he hurt his foot I had to do it all while he rode into Powell and got the doctor to fix things for him. Two days I had to do it all after he got back because he couldn't hardly walk."

Frank spoke for the first time since the packer had followed them to camp. "I didn't know they had a doctor down in Powell."

Jess Spooner looked away from Skye when he answered. "Neither did we, but we seen the rooftops from a long way east and Cal's foot was giving him . . . was hurting him a lot, so he rode in."

Skye used this diversion to move closer to the little fire ring, and when Jess Spooner decided it was time to leave and smiled in her direction, she smiled back, then got busy.

Frank saw the marshal and his posse-men making camp slightly apart from the packers' camp and about equal distant from the Cameron ranch camp. When the twig fire was burning he forgot about the possemen and the packers, knelt to help with the meal, and was gently shouldered aside by Skye. Sam and Fred grinned without showing that they had noticed.

Rand and Carl came in from caring for the animals. The coffee was hot, and they each drew off a cup and sat down. Dusk arrived while the pale smoke from three separate cooking fires was rising straight up because there was no air moving.

For the circumstances, the Cameron riders had a pleasant camp. No one was particularly tired and nothing was said about the earlier confrontation. Having finished eating before full darkness arrived, they talked a little and were having more coffee when the packers arrived.

Jess Spooner grinned as usual and his part-ner nodded and showed less smile and more uncertainty. He too had a dark beard. He was about the same size and heft as Spooner, but he was more circumspect as he sat down and thanked Sam for the cup of coffee held out toward him, acknowledging all the introductions with a quick, birdlike nod of his head.

He stretched his right boot toward the fire and Spooner said, "Mule stepped on it. The doctor down at Powell fixed him up with a danged leather sock. Show 'em, Cal."

Cal got red in the face and glared at his partner. "Drink your coffee," he said sharply.

Fred was interested. "I never heard of such a thing. Leather stocking? Does it work?"

Cal glanced at his outstretched foot. "Yeah. In fact when I walk on it, it don't hardly hurt at all. . . . That doctor said he fitted out a lot of men with them things back during the war." Cal had been drawn out a little and began to loosen up. He did not smile, in fact he never did smile. He wiggled the foot a little, watching the movement as he also said, "He was a good hand. They'd had a shootin' a couple of days before and he'd been trying like the devil to save the town marshal's life. . . . He died in the morning and I rode in just before sundown. I guess the doctor'd been as busy as a boxful of kittens, but the feller died anyway."

Everyone was looking straight at Cal. There was not a sound. He glanced up, saw their stares, and raised the tin cup to drain it. As he put it aside he leaned to arise as he said,

"Obliged for the java. Jess, we better get back to camp."

Frank stopped them both. "Just a minute. The town marshal down at Powell is dead?"

Cal nodded. "That's what the doctor told me."

"Did he tell you how it happened?"

Cal fidgeted. "Well, he said some fellers come into town and commenced raisin' hell. The constable went out to stop them, and they shot him out in the center of the roadway."

An almost audible sigh passed among the listeners. Jess Spooner looked from face to face, bewildered and troubled. "Something wrong?" he asked.

Frank bypassed the question. "Earlier, when that feller from our party rode up and talked to you, did you tell him the town marshal down at Powell had been killed?"

Cal shook his head. "No. Didn't have no reason to. He wanted to know where we come from an' I told him. From over northeast of here, a settlement called Grant's Ferry. He asked if we'd mind if you folks camped here. I told him we wouldn't mind at all. . . . I had work to do so I went over and commenced doing it." Cal stared at Frank Cutler, obviously sensing something. "There's something wrong, ain't there?"

Again Frank bypassed the question. "When that feller talked to you, did he say anything about us — about his friends over yonder, or about the rest of us — what we're doing out here or where we're going?"

Cal's answer was low. "No. All that was said between us was just what I told you. I didn't ask no questions. Like I said, I had work to do. Seventeen head of livestock for just two men don't leave a lot of time for jawing when camp's got to be set up, mister."

Frank looked around among the blank faces. Every eye was on the packer. He looked back and said, "Cal, don't neither of you mention to those men over yonder that you were anywhere near Powell, let alone that one of you rode in down there. Don't mention the dead marshal."

Cal's eyes were perfectly round in the firelight. He did not say a word, but his partner did. "Why? What the hell is this all about?"

Frank thought about his reply before offering it. "That big feller over there, the last one to ride in and help the others make camp . . . He's wearing a town marshal's badge and told us he was the marshal down at Powell."

Cal stared at Frank, but again it was Jess Spooner who spoke. "Why? Why would a man do something like that?"

Frank hung fire a moment before answering. He was beginning to have an idea why Hanford had done that, but that was all it was — an idea. "I don't know," he replied to the packer. Then he pointed to Sam. "He put my partner there and me under arrest for a shooting that happened down there over a month ago. He said he was taking us down there to stand trial."

Cal's expression underwent a sudden change. "Wait a minute, mister. Was that the saloon fight when three freighters got killed?"

"Yes."

"Well . . . The doctor told me that was a fair fight. He said everyone called it a fair fight, an' the two fellers lit out afterwards." Cal scrambled to his feet and stood hipshot favoring his injured foot. "We better get back and see about the mules," he said swiftly to his partner. As they were turning Frank had one more thing to add to what he had already told them. "If you go over to the other camp, don't mention anything you told us. And don't let them know you were ever in Powell."

Cal's retort was short and vehement. "Mister, we ain't going nowhere near that camp. . . . Good night, ma'am."

CHAPTER 17

By Starlight

Without speaking, Rand dug around until he found a pony of whiskey, then refilled his tin cup, laced it, and raised his eyes to Frank as he passed over the bottle. "If he ain't the marshal, then who is he?"

Frank accepted the bottle and also laced a refilled cup. "I don't know who he is, who any of them are."

Sam spoke up. "But you got an idea, Frank, just like I have."

The others passed coffee and the little bottle around while awaiting Frank's response. Skye alone among them had neither whiskey nor coffee.

Frank was not sure. He would have preferred saying nothing but they were waiting, so he spoke. "The Powell town marshal, before this last one, was killed in the saloon doorway by a party of freighters. I don't know any more about it than that. When I rode in there was a big storm. I was looking for shelter. Over at the saloon Sam here was having a drink by himself. Some freighters came in looking for trouble. They started a fight with Sam. Three against one. I bought in. . . . When it was over there were three dead freighters, Sam had been winged, and we got the hell out of there. I never saw the marshal; didn't even know they had one until the packer told us a while ago. . . . From here on I'm guessing. According to the widow woman of the marshal those freighters shot, it was a big band of them. The men who picked a fight with Sam and me, just three men, scairt hell out of the barman when they entered the saloon. . . . My guess is that the three we shot it out with were most likely part of that same mob." Frank jerked his head. "My guess is that is who those men are. . . . I'd say that barman recognized those three. I'd guess they were part of the mob that shot down the widow woman's husband in the saloon doorway. . . . I think they got at least one good tracker among them. . . . They found Sam and me, and . . . "

"And," said Carl coldly, "you want to know why I think they never told them packers anything? Because they never had any intention of you and Sam reaching Powell."

A moment of silence followed what Carl had said. The men sipped laced coffee and considered the little cooking fire, their faces reflecting solemn, inward thoughts.

Skye spoke, finally. "We outnumber them."

No one commented about that. In fact no one had anything to say until Rand Belton flung away the dregs of his coffee and pulled grass to swab out the cup. "I'll tell you something," he exclaimed. "When they rode into the yard I knew they wasn't range men, and not just because of the flat heels on their boots." Rand stopped speaking and shoved the clean cup into a saddlebag. He did not elaborate. In fact he did not speak again for a long while.

Skye went directly to the point. "What do we do?"

Carl and Fred gazed at her. They had not worked as long as Rand had for the Cameron ranch, but each had been there for more than one season, and this was the first time either of them had heard her say anything like that. She *told* people what to do, she did not *ask* them.

She was watching Frank's profile in firelight. He shrugged his thick shoulders. "We don't go down to Powell. I guess we'd all agree about that."

Carl was through reflecting. He never reflected for very long anyway, about anything. "Walk over there, throw down on them, and kick out a few answers."

Mack regarded Carl. "Then what?"

Carl flashed an annoyed look back. "How would I know?"

Sam turned to Skye. "Where is my gun?"

She turned to unbuckle the pocket flaps of the saddle she was using as a backrest, drew out the weapon, and handed it over. Then she said, "It's not loaded," and Sam went to work plugging in loads from his belt. When he flipped the gate closed he looked across at Carl. "I'm ready."

But Carl did not budge. He was waiting for Frank to speak. It was a long wait, and before he could speak one of their horses snorted. Frank turned. There was starlight and little more because the moon was no more than one-quarter full. Frank arose facing southward. No one else moved. He walked out a short distance, saw the shadow of a man leading an animal, and altered course to make an interception. It was Jess Spooner leading a large mule. Jess halted, squinted, then said, "Mister Cutler?"

Frank went closer. The burly, bearded man was wearing a six-gun, something neither he nor his partner had been doing earlier. Jess said, "We're leaving. I'm not strong on travelin' at night with a packtrain, but I'm a hell of a lot less strong on settin' atop a dynamite keg."

Frank returned to the fire circle, explained what he had been told, then dug out his makings and rolled a smoke. Eventually he looked at the wide-awake faces turned in his direction. "That might be a good idea. Head back for the yard."

Carl spat aside, his face showing rank disgust. "And what about them fellers who was going to hang you and Sam? Just let them go on their way like nothing ever happened?"

Frank blew smoke and regarded Carl across the embers. "We couldn't just walk up on them, Carl. They're sweating as much as we are. They're alert too."

"Walk up anyway," the short man said.

Sam interposed a comment. "Set them afoot, Frank. Run off their horses, then just set here until dawn. Being afoot whittles everyone down a lot."

Rand Belton had been listening, and now made his own thoughts known. "We outnumber them. If we surround their camp they're not going to start anything."

One thing was clear to Frank. Whether or not he preferred prudence to its alternative, the others didn't. He pitched the cigarette into the fire and said, "All right. But not now. Not until a lot later, when the packers have gone and everyone should be asleep." He met Carl's flinty look, then regarded the other men. They seemed agreeable but none of them said so.

Frank stood up. "I'll take the first watch."

But Carl was opposed to that also. "I'll do it. You can take a turn when it's time for us to go over there."

Everyone but Carl, Frank, and Skye headed for their blanket rolls. Frank stood in the pleasant night until Skye came over and said, "Walk out a ways."

They went westerly, and from farther back they could distinguish the sounds of unhappy mules moving around as they were being loaded. Skye stared a long time in the direction of the Hanford camp.

"Would they really do all this because you killed some of their friends?"

Frank thought they would. "The ones we shot it out with were the kind of men who would, so I guess these other ones are too."

"But I prefer your suggestion, Frank. We

could be back at the yard a little after day-break. They wouldn't follow."

He looked down. "I think they would. They've gone to all the trouble of tracking Sam and me up here. Skye, they're not going to just turn back now."

She held out something in the darkness. It was the Colt Lightning she carried inside her shirt. He did not raise a hand. "Keep it. You might want it."

"You're unarmed, Frank."

At this particular moment that did not worry him. "I don't like the idea of you being here, Skye. You shouldn't have come."

"If we hadn't, by now you and Sam would probably have been shot in the back." She put the double-action six-gun back inside her shirt. "Frank, it's hard to believe. I never liked Hanford, or his surly possemen, but I never doubted but that he was a lawman."

Frank could have echoed that. Instead he turned and reached for her hand. They walked out farther, until even the faint sound of the packers at work was lost to them. He turned, released her fingers and said, "Mind if I tell you something?"

She answered without hesitation. "Not at all."

At the last moment his courage failed him.

"Well, sure is a nice night, isn't it?"

She did not examine the sky as he was now doing. Nor did she reply to his comment. She reached with a stiff forefinger and tapped his chest. When his head came down she said, "Why should I mind if you told me something like that?"

He pulled in a deep breath. "It wasn't what I was going to tell you."

"What were you going to tell me?"

He did not rush to answer. He had known women casually now and then. Mostly, he could not even remember their names. For years he had been a solitary individual. Up until he had ridden into Powell to escape a storm. After that it seemed that whatever fate or destiny, or something anyway, had control of such things, had pushed people at him. First Sam and now Skye Cameron. Other people as well; freighters, an embittered widow, outlaws, and the vengeful possemen from Powell.

He had not really disliked having most of this happen. He had never really liked being a solitary individual. He had never regretted partnering with Sam, and he did not regret meeting Skye. It always came back to her.

"Well," he said, starting out slowly. "I was

207

going to tell you that I never liked a woman like I do you."

He watched for her reaction with a dubious expression on his face.

She kept looking at him. For a while she had no answer but finally she spoke. "Frank, I didn't like you. And I was wrong about you. I told you that." Her green eyes assumed an expression of teasing and in a deeper voice she mimicked him. "Mind if I tell you something?"

He waited.

"I like you. . . . You are one of those people who don't intrude; you keep getting bigger and taller and stronger all the time." She paused, but he still stood looking at her. "Do you want Rand's job when we get home?"

He shifted his position a little. Inwardly, he had not expected her to say that. He was uncertain what he had expected, but it was not that. "Let's wait and see if we get back home. Then maybe we can talk about that." He looked past her. "I expect we'd ought to go back now."

For a while as they paced along together she watched the ground, then she looked up. "I'm not timid, Frank. I've never been timid. . . . But you make me that way. For some damned reason I can't get my thoughts out the way I want to express them."

He looked at her, smiling. "Exactly the way I feel."

"Well . . . ?"

"We better get back."

CHAPTER 18

A Cold Gun Barrel

Before he dozed off he listened to the pack-train lining out westerly. Before dusk he had admired the mules. They were large, strong-boned animals. None of them were above ten years of age and they had been properly cared for. He had not seen a gall nor a too-long hoof. The kind of men who would pay what it would cost to buy that kind of quality mule would be the kind of men who would care for them.

He wondered sleepily what Hanford — if that was his name — and his companions thought about the mule train pulling out in the middle of the night. Then he slept.

It did not seem that he had slept very long when he was awakened by something cold pressing against his throat. It was a six-gun barrel lying sideways. Above it in the ghostly night gloom was a set of thick, coarse features. Beyond, dimly discernible and watching, were three other shadows, each pointing a six-gun at him. The night was utterly silent. From the corner of his eye he could see other slumbering bodies scattered close by. The man kneeling above him whispered.

"Not a sound. Not one damned sound . . . Now then, sit up . . . easy and quiet."

Frank pushed slowly upward. The coarse-featured man leaned back a little and kept his gun pointing. Behind him a familiar voice told Frank to ease up out of the bedroll and put on his boots. This time it was Bill Hanford who spoke.

Frank obeyed, his mind absolutely clear. He got to his feet and Hanford murmured to a man at his side. "Get the other one. Brain him if he needs it."

Frank turned just his head. There was supposed to be a sentinel somewhere around. Hanford stepped close and whispered about that. "He ain't going to help you. He got hit over the head." Hanford turned as the man sent to awaken Sam knelt and pushed his six-gun within inches of Sam's face.

Frank hoped with all his heart that Sam would not come up fighting. If he did, and roused the others, the massacre would begin.

They all watched in motionless stillness. Sam awakened and started to sit up. The posseman with the gun whispered to him and put the pistol barrel within inches of Sam's face. Surprise and shock held Sam motionless long enough for him to see the others and Frank standing nearby. He obeyed each order the posseman gave him, and when he was over beside Frank, Hanford motioned for them to precede him in the direction of the possemen's camp. They did not make a sound.

Over there, Frank and Sam saw their own horses saddled, bridled, and waiting. Camp had been struck. There was nothing on the ground now to indicate anyone had camped there, except the cooling char of a dying fire which gave off no light.

He and Sam exchanged a look. One of the possemen was standing near a patient horse examining Sam's ivory-stocked six-gun, and when they were ready to ride, he put Sam's gun in his holster and his own weapon in his nearside saddlebag.

It worked as well as any redskin ambush had ever worked. There was summer grass underfoot to deaden sounds, and Hanford led off riding at a walk. They went due east in the direction of the stage road. The night was cold, the moon was gone — Frank guessed it was about one or two o'clock in the morning — and there was a posseman between the prisoners. He and Sam had not been tied; no one had dropped a rope over the heads of their animals either. Those things would probably come later when the party was well along on its way. But there was no way to break away and run for it, not even in the velvet darkness. The horse had never been foaled who could outrun a bullet.

He turned toward the posseman and said, "I guess you boys didn't sleep last night."

At first it seemed the posseman was disinclined to reply, but eventually he did. When he answered he also turned a venomous glare upon Cutler. "We never figured to sleep. An' we had to wait until them packers left. That was good luck, them leaving. Otherwise, we'd have had to wait until tomorrow night . . . but we'd have got it done, you can bet your last dollar on that."

Frank considered the man. He was a surly, compactly built individual and back at the ranch yard he had said the least of any of the possemen. It was not difficult to appreciate that when he made up his mind to do something, nothing short of a bullet would stop him.

"Why?" Frank asked, and got no answer.

The surly man did not look around again. He rode hunched into his coat as though Frank did not exist.

Sam was on the left side of the surly rider. Beyond him was the youngest of the posse-men, a lanky, slab-sided individual barely into his twenties. He had a pock-scarred face and a bitter cast to his mouth. Sam made one effort to start a conversation and did not get even as far as Frank had with the surly man. The lanky rider glanced once at Sam and did not look at him again.

Bill Hanford rode steadily through the coldest part of the night. When they reached the road he crossed it and kept on riding. He knew where he was going. Once or twice he looked back. Otherwise he led the way and seemed concerned only with where they were going.

With the arrival of false dawn it was possible to make out an occasional tree, usually a lowland pine, but after Hanford altered course slightly, riding easterly on a tangent, infrequent stands of dark-barked fir trees appeared. They were heading into some distant foothills and Frank suspected that once they were hidden back in there, the shooting would begin.

Dawn came, cold and slate-colored. Hanford continued toward the brakes. The sun arrived, spreading an enormous splash of brilliance outward and downward and Hanford reached the foothills.

Frank glanced back. For as far as he could see the land was empty. Bill Hanford knew the countryside; he was evidently also a good planner. His scheme had worked perfectly. By now of course back at the Cameron camp their disappearance had been discovered, and no doubt Mack had saddled first to take up the eastward trail. Hanford had obviously considered these things.

They did not halt until the sun was climbing. There was no appreciable warmth and probably would not be for another two hours. The place where Hanford finally drew rein and dismounted had a number of uneven, grassy, low hills between it and the rearward open country. There was thick underbrush, in some places as tall as a mounted man. There were also more fir trees than pines up in here. Under less worrisome circumstances Sam would have recognized this area for what it was, a haven for blood-sucking wood ticks, and would not have permitted his horse to brush against any of the undergrowth.

Hanford was removing his roping gloves when he said, "Get down."

Sam and Frank swung to the ground beside their animals. The possemen had assembled behind them and also dismounted. Frank and Sam had the three bleak men behind and Bill Hanford in front.

For a few moments the only sound was of drowsy, disturbed birds roosting in the underbrush. They made sleepy protests. Then Bill Hanford took the badge he had been wearing from a coat pocket, held it out to be seen, then contemptuously flung it into the underbrush.

Frank said, "If we're supposed to be surprised, we're not."

Hanford unbuttoned his coat and swept it back on the right side. "No? Why not?"

"Because those packers told us last night that the marshal in Powell was killed in the roadway some time ago."

Hanford stared at Frank for a long time. Behind the prisoners the other men also stared. Eventually, Hanford said, "If you knew that, why did you bed down last night as if there wasn't nothing wrong?"

"To wait for daylight."

Hanford smiled thinly. "That was foolish."

Frank could perhaps have agreed, but he did not. Instead, he said, "Since you aren't lawmen, who are you?"

"Well sir," replied Hanford. "That was goin' to be the last thing we talked about. But since you want to get out of the way soon, I'm agreeable. . . . You see that husky feller behind you, and the tall one with the scarred face? And you remember those three men you killed down in Powell? Those gents behind you was related to those other fellers. . . . The young feller was the son of one of them, and the other man was the brother of another one. . . . Me and the other gent behind you, we'd partnered with those men for a long time."

Sam said, "Freighters?"

Hanford had ignored Sam up until now. When his gaze drifted away from Cutler to Sam, it darkened. "Boy . . . you son of a bitch . . . I'm goin' to teach you a lesson you'll never forget, not even after you've gone to hell."

Hanford stopped speaking. He did not move his eyes away from Sam as he began to shrug out of his riding coat. Where it fell in the grass he also dropped his six-gun. Frank knew what to expect. Anyone who had been in the Cameron yard when Sam and the large blacksmith had tangled would have known, but none of these men had witnessed that battle. With the exception of Bill Hanford, they were savagely smiling, enjoying in advance what they were sure was about to happen.

Hanford wasted time preparing for battle because he was enjoying every second of this. Sam watched, so did Frank. Hanford shed his hat and dropped it atop the gun, then he stood wide-legged, rolling up his sleeves. He was a large, powerful man, larger and heavier than Sam Morton; but the blacksmith had been even larger, and he had also been more powerfully built.

Hanford had lost his smile. He finished with the sleeves while holding his head back so that he could look down his nose at young Sam. Then he killed another few moments standing there staring. He did not speak and just glared downward as though to intimidate Sam. The younger man looked back. In a mild voice as he shed his coat and hat, Sam said, "I'd as soon not do this, Mister Hanford," and the onlookers behind Sam laughed.

Hanford did not respond; he started forward. Frank was to one side. He moved even more to one side, in the direction of Hanford's coat and hat on the ground.

Hanford would have been a formidable opponent even if he had not been so confident. What he saw in front of him was a younger man, taffy-haired, sinewy, and not his match in size, heft, or experience. When he got too close Sam gave ground. Behind him that lanky younger man swore and said, "Stand up and fight, you bastard."

Hanford continued to advance, slowly and inexorably, his large, stonelike fists raised. Sam shuffled as though to retreat again and Hanford lunged at him, struck savagely into empty air, and whirled to face the younger man on his left side. He did not realize that Sam had gone to the left because Hanford was right-handed, and in order to hit hard he would have to turn completely to his left. Hanford lunged and struck with his left. Sam slipped the awkward left-handed blow over one shoulder and came in beneath it, hit Hanford three times, twice in the soft parts, and once higher, up alongside his cheek and temple.

Suddenly, there was not a sound from the freighters. Hanford's arms went down to protect his stomach. Sam shifted his attack farther to the left and peppered Hanford, then he moved back and straightened up to wait.

The surly, compact freighter said, "God . . . damn," in an awed whisper, and Frank shifted another few inches closer to the coat and hat on the ground behind him.

Bill Hanford had paid for his overconfidence. It required several moments for him to recover from the low blows, and he stared at Sam as he straightened slightly and brought up his arms. Now, when he started forward, he did so with a murderous resolve, but he also moved more slowly and was no longer moving flat down on his feet. He balanced forward.

Sam remained stationary, arms at his sides, eyes fixed upon the older man. He was not even breathing hard. It may have been the wisdom born of pain and caution that made Hanford halt out of reach, or it may have been the way Sam was not moving, just staring at him. But whatever inspired Hanford to feint left, then right, did not advance his cause very much because although Sam turned slightly each time, he was never off-balance as Hanford expected him to be.

He said, "Boy . . . you son of a bitch . . . I'm going to kill you!"

Sam did not open his mouth; he dropped forward slightly and started to stalk the big freighter. To Frank, who had seen this identical maneuver before, the battle was nearing its climax and end. He eyed the staring, engrossed freighters then shifted again closer to the coat and hat on the ground.

Sam baited Hanford, but the freighter was

too wary to lunge, so Sam smiled straight into the larger man's face and went quickly to the left again, but close enough this time to make the temptation too great. Hanford gathered himself, sank flat down on both feet, and charged, arms wide, hands bent like talons.

Frank did not breathe. Neither did the three men southward of him. Hanford caught shirt cloth in both hands. His sweaty, beet red face glowed as he started to pull the younger man to him.

Sam hit him just above the belt buckle. He hit him even harder above the heart, and the last time he fired his balled right hand he had been pulled inward almost too close for the strike to be effective. It splashed claret from the big man's broken mouth.

Hanford's hands loosened, his body sagged, and evidently instinct told him to back away, but he was already getting numb as he started to move, and he stumbled. He did not go down, but neither could he defend himself. He hung there with his eyes no longer focusing and with blood spilling down his shirt front.

Frank made his dive.

The three possemen were stone-still in total disbelief. Possibly they had seen Bill Hanford in other brawls; but whether this was what held them motionless in shock, or whether it was the fact that Hanford had been so totally out-fought by a youth half his age and at least fifty pounds lighter who could not possibly have been as experienced, they had their eyes fixed on the wavering big man.

CHAPTER 19

An Unplanned Ending

Frank had knocked the hat aside and was closing his fingers around the gun when the lanky, pock-faced freighter yelped and grabbed frantically for his hip holster.

The two older freighters tensed into a crouch, their attention wrenched away from Bill Hanford by the younger man's cry. It was too late.

Frank rolled, saw the lanky man's gun rising, stopped rolling, and shot him. He then started to roll again, even before the lanky man leaned forward looking surprised.

Only Bill Hanford did not move; he did not appear to realize what was happening as Sam faded from in front. Sam ran a shifting pattern then dove head first into the grass, but the two remaining freighters were aiming frantically at Frank. They did not look in

Sam's direction. If they had they might have seen something else: Bill Hanford started to fall, very slowly at first, then he gathered momentum like a tree and by the time he struck the ground, hard, he was as limp as a sack of wet grain.

The compact, surly freighter fired twice, two very fast and inaccurate snap shots, then turned and raced toward the nearest clump of thick underbrush. The other freighter was bent low with his feet spread wide, trying to focus his front sight on Frank, who did not roll in a direct line, but whipped left and right. The freighter fired. Dirt and grass erupted where Frank had been, not where he was, and this was Frank's split-second opportunity. It required a second to haul back the dog of a single-action six-gun and another second to squeeze the trigger.

Frank stopped rolling, came half way up off the ground with his cocked Colt swinging, and fired. The leaning freighter was punched back upright. His gun went off and earth exploded fifteen feet in front. Frank fired again and the man went over backwards with both arms pinwheeling. He landed on his back and rolled just once.

The surly man was hidden when he fired and missed by half a yard. Frank rolled to the left, jumped up, and sprinted. The invisible freighter fired again and missed again.

Frank reached dense scrub brush and felt nothing as thorns ripped at him. He worked his way in deeper and to his right. Then he sank down upon some pebbly earth and panted, trying to locate Sam. There was no sign of him. If he had also reached the screening underbrush, it had to have been over among the thickets that also hid the remaining freighter.

There was silence deep enough to reach out and touch. Where sun brilliance flooded the clearing, two dead men were lying not far apart, one on his side with an arm under his head as though sleeping, and the other flat on his back with both arms flung wide.

Hanford had not moved after falling face-down in the trampled grass.

Frank shook sweat off and used bullets from his shell belt to reload Hanford's weapon. Then he got belly-down where the trunks but not many of the branches of the underbrush shadowed the earth, and he waited.

But evidently the surly man was doing the same, because there was no more gunfire.

Frank worried about Sam who was un-armed over there. Any sound at all would draw fire from the freighter.

Their horses had fled a hundred yards down the opening toward open country when the first gunshot had panicked them. But, being horses, they were now cropping grass as though terror had not panicked them moments before.

Frank wiped blood off the back of his left hand which had been scratched during his rush into the underbrush. He was filthy, his shirttail was out, the garment was torn in many places, and although his heartbeat was subsiding, he was still sucking air.

And he continued to wait, until it occurred to him that his antagonist over yonder could, by taking plenty of time, work his way southward with the underbrush concealing his progress, until he was parallel with the horses. He would have to expose himself when he left the underbrush for the open glade where the animals were, but he would also be well beyond accurate six-gun range.

Frank got to his knees and considered the brush on his left. There were tiny varmint trails, but he could not use them so he arose and began zigzagging northward until he found infrequent, and often blind-end, crooked passageways.

It required time to make progress this way, but he did not want that surviving freighter to escape. He had perspiration running in tiny rivulets under his shirt and downward from his forehead. There was heat now, but more than heat made a man sweat like that.

A light breeze swept up through the slot where the freighters had intended to shoot Sam and Frank. It was no more than ankle-high, but it helped cool the area. Then Frank lost it entirely when he reached the easterly brush thickets and began working his way down through them.

He found fresh boot tracks, guessed they had been left by Sam, and followed them, but warily. In this kind of ground cover two men usually met suddenly and at close range.

Without warning a gun sounded not far ahead and tiny leaves and limbs broke and scattered a yard to Frank's right. He sank to one knee, waiting, but there was no second shot, and he did not believe the freighter had been firing at him.

He stood up and called out. "Sam! Leave him be! I've got his range! Don't get between us!"

Sam heard him, even the distant horses flung up their heads, and that meant the freighter had also heard him.

The underbrush was less dense as Frank moved cautiously southward. He had to stop twice to drag the slippery palm of his gunhand down a trouser leg to dry it before regripping Hanford's gun.

The freighter had to realize he was being stalked, that he had no support, that he was up against a man who could kill with a handgun while rolling in the grass, and that the moment he rushed forth to try and catch a horse, he would become a target. He also had to know that Sam was trying to locate him too, and whether he thought Sam was still unarmed or not, he had seen what Sam could do without a weapon.

Frank would have been content to make the man sweat himself into a mood of total, debilitating fear if it had not been for the horses. He continued working his way through underbrush, veering westward closer to the clearing when there was no other way, and once he paused over there to look at the horses.

The moment the freighter broke from cover, the horses would see him and fling up their heads, and if he made the underbrush quiver the horses would also detect that and stare. They would give the man away before he could reach them.

Frank gauged the distance, moved another few yards southward, reassessed the distance, then looked about for a suitable place to wait.

He was within much better handgun range. It was a long wait. Unless the surly man was a complete fool, although he was now down there with the horses tantalizingly within reach, he had to be aware that Frank Cutler was also very close. If Cutler was too close, then trying to run out and catch a horse could be final and fatal.

Cutler had been on the same side of the clearing when he had called to his partner, which meant Cutler was coming toward him.

The sun was still climbing. Some deerflies came into the underbrush, and the birds which had been gone a long time returned to hover, then sped away again as a man's hoarse outcry rose from the southward underbrush.

"Cutler . . . You hear me, Cutler?"

"I hear you. Go out and catch yourself a horse!"

"I quit. I give up. You hear me?"

Frank raised a filthy cuff to push off sweat. "Walk out into the clearing. Hold the gun over your head and walk out there."

Silence settled for a long time. Another shout from southward shattered it. "I walk out there with a gun in my hand and you're goin' to shoot me, Cutler."

"If you *don't* walk out with your gun, I'm

229

going to shoot you. Walk . . . Walk out into plain sight!"

But the freighter did not appear. He said, "I need your word — no more shooting."

Frank turned at a faint rustling of underbrush and saw Sam moving in his direction. He called back to the freighter. "This is the last time. . . . *Walk out there!*"

"Naw . . . not without your word, Cutler."

"You have my word."

Sam leaned past some thorny little wiry limbs and grinned. Frank grinned back then swung to watch the horses. They were standing utterly still, heads up and ears pointing. Frank drew up both knees, rested his left forearm atop them, placed his right hand atop the forearm, cocked Hanford's six-gun, and waited.

The compactly built freighter shoved past his sheltering thicket and hovered, looking northward as he raised both arms. The man's fear disgusted Frank. "You damned fool, walk away from the brush. . . . If I wanted to kill you I could do it now, even with the brush beside you. Walk on out there."

The freighter finally appeared in full view walking in the direction of the animals. He stopped when the horses appeared about to turn and run southward again.

Frank stood up and beat off dust, little brown leaves, and soil, holstered the Hanford gun, and moved out of the underbrush. He started down there, never once taking his eyes off the burly man with the six-gun in his right hand above his head. When Frank halted they were less than ten yards apart. He studied the brutish, greasy features of the surly man and said, "Now is your chance."

The freighter flung his six-gun away without lowering his hands. "I told you — I quit."

"Put your arms down and walk back up there ahead of me. . . . What's your name?"

"Ellis."

"Keep walking, Ellis. . . . You and Hanford are all that's left. You want a good look at the others?"

"No!"

"What did Hanford have in mind when he rode up in here?"

"Beat your partner half to death, then shoot the pair of you."

Sam was out there with Bill Hanford leaning against one of Sam's legs, holding a canteen so Hanford could drink. He spilled much more than he could swallow. His lips were split and so swollen his entire face looked lopsided. Deerflies had been attracted by blood and hovered in small swarms.

As Ellis walked up he eyed the canteen greedily, then asked Sam if he could have a drink. Sam passed over the canteen, turned and walked down where the two dead men were, picked up his heirloom six-gun, and walked back.

He held up his hands toward Frank. They had not been entirely healed from his fight in the ranch yard, and now they were bloody and puffed up again.

Frank took the canteen, drank deeply, and handed it to Sam with some advice. "Trickle cold water over them. With someone like Hanford you never know but what you'll get an infection." He gestured toward Hanford. "Get up."

The large man arose with some assistance from Ellis. He was steady on his feet but left Frank with the feeling that a slight push would send him down again. They regarded each other for a moment before Hanford said something which was indistinguishable. Frank said, "Where is my gun?" Hanford pointed down in the direction of the horses and mumbled again. Frank did not turn to look down there. "I think I'll kill you, Hanford. That's what you figured to do to us. It'd be justified."

Ellis's perpetually narrowed eyes widened.

"He ain't armed, for Chris'sake."

"Neither were we when you brought us up in here to be shot."

"Mister Cutler . . ."

"Find him a gun, Ellis. Go get one off that scar-faced feller."

The horrified freighter did not move. "Mister Cutler . . . he ain't in no condition to face you. . . . You can't just up and murder a man."

"Why can't I? You sons of bitches were going to. What's the difference?"

Ellis swallowed with an effort and could not take his eyes off Frank's face.

Sam spoke from behind the pair of freighters. "Riders, Frank."

All four of them turned to look far southward where five horsemen had appeared riding slowly behind Mack, who was out front reading sign for the others.

Skye was directly behind Mack. Fred, Rand, and Carl were behind Skye. They finally saw the four men on foot watching them approach, and Mack straightened in the saddle.

The sun was directly above, there was no shade in the clearing and it was thin around the trees and throughout the thickets of underbrush. It was hot out there, as Frank reached for the canteen and drank again, and then offered it to Hanford.

Carl and Rand rounded up the loose horses and brought them along, well behind Mack and Skye.

CHAPTER 20

Tired Men — and Horses

The Cameron riders swung off and stared. The area resembled a *matanza*, a slaughter yard. Skye brought Frank the almost depleted pony of whiskey and until he had taken two swallows she said nothing, then she handed the bottle to Sam and turned with her hand hooked around Frank's arm. She took him in search of shade, of which there was almost none. Behind them Carl leaned across the seat of his saddle and gazed at Hanford and the surly man while Rand and Mack went over to hobble the horses, before joining Fred who was staring at the dead freighters.

Carl said, "No oak trees around here."

Hanford and Ellis understood the implication. Oak limbs grew outward from the trunk; they made excellent hanging trees. Pines and fir trees did not.

"Which one of you hit our sentry over the head last night?"

Hanford had a hand raised to brush the flies away from his smashed mouth and blood-stiff shirt front. Ellis had to reply because Hanford either could not or would not. Ellis jutted his jaw in Indian fashion in the direction of the scar-faced dead man. "Him. That lanky feller over yonder."

Carl spat. "Sure he did. A man don't have to be very bright to blame dead folks, does he?"

"It's the truth," exclaimed Ellis.

Carl considered the large man. "Who beat him like that?"

"Morton," replied Ellis.

Carl grinned. It was the first time he'd done that in a long while. "Wish I'd been here to see it. . . . What was you going to do with Cutler and Morton after you snuck 'em away from our camp last night?"

Ellis took a moment to mop off sweat with a soiled blue bandana. "Shoot 'em."

Carl continued to lean and stare. He probably would have spoken again but Rand called from over where the dead freighters were lying, and Carl turned, taking his horse with him as he walked over there.

Rand spoke dispassionately. "I was telling

236

Mack and Fred I'm leaving now."

Carl looked up in surprise.

Rand shrugged. "I told the boss I would quit when we got back, but hell, there wouldn't be no point in me going back. . . . This here mess is over. It came out right, I guess. . . . She don't need me any more, and I guess I don't need Cameron ranch any more."

Carl scowled. "What the hell are you talking about? You're the foreman, Rand."

Belton put a scornful gaze upon the shorter man. "You're blind, Carl," he said, then turned brisk. "Let's get these fellers tied over their saddles and get the hell out of here. . . . Fred, you and Mack lend me a hand. Carl, fetch up their animals."

The men had plenty to occupy their minds as they worked, so very little was said, even after they had shrouded the corpses in their own blankets and had lashed them like salt sacks so that they would not work loose and fall.

The horses were thirsty and fidgeted a lot and that brought curses as well as understanding. It was when they helped Hanford over his saddle that Fred showed Ellis the sticky hair beneath his hat where a swelling had appeared last night after he had been hit over the head.

Normally, Fred was almost diffident, but

not now. He asked the same question Carl had asked and got the same answer.

"It was that pock-faced feller you fellers tied on the bay horse."

Carl was within hearing distance and growled. "He's lying, Fred. I'll bet you a new hat on it."

Hanford mouthed difficult words. "It is the truth."

They all looked up at Hanford's smashed lower face, then let this topic die as they continued to work, but now in silence.

Frank and Skye came out of the brush toward them, and this added a fresh distraction. Carl leaned on a horse solemnly eyeing them, then sighed and went back to work.

Everything had been done; they were ready to ride. Skye accepted the reins Fred held out and Frank got his reins from Sam, who had been listening a lot and saying nothing while the range man had been working. When they were in the saddle and ready, Rand motioned for Sam to ride up with him in the lead, and they moved at a dead walk down the slot of green toward open country. Rand wanted to hear about the fight. Before Sam was finished, Carl and Mack were close by also listening.

Ellis had draped the nearly depleted canteen around Hanford's saddle horn and from time to time the large man poured water into a cupped hand and held it to his mouth.

They reached open country and turned back over their own tracks, heading southwesterly with the sun slanting slightly off-center. Rand halted beside the stage road and without a word or glance at his companions, turned back to seek Skye and Frank. He nodded to Frank and asked Skye to ride aside with him for a way. Carl led off across the road as they moved out again.

Rand was a blunt man. "If you got any money along, you can pay me off now. If not, you can mail it to me down in New Messico. . . . If I rode all the way back, I'd just have to pack my war bag then come back down this way. . . . You won't need me to ramrod the gather anyway. . . . Is this all right with you?"

She thought about asking him if this was really what he wanted, but she didn't, and for a good reason. She knew Rand Belton. If he said he was leaving now, asking him not to would change nothing.

"I'll have to mail you the money, Rand. I guess Carl can box your war bag and mail that too. . . . I'm sorry to see you go."

For a moment they looked at one another, then he turned away. "When I get down there

I'll send you an address."

She nodded. "Good luck, Rand, and thank you for a lot of things."

He did not smile. He rarely did that, but his flinty dark eyes mirrored an uncharacteristic soft wistfulness very briefly, then he reined away and with his horse at a lope, widened the distance between them without once looking back.

Skye returned to Frank Cutler's side in the drag of the cavalcade and related what had transpired. Frank rolled a smoke and lit up, squinted down where Rand Belton was already growing small as he rode out of their lives, and could not honestly say he was sorry to see Belton go.

There was almost none of the customary idle talk. Up front, Carl and Sam bit off cuds from the same plug while Mack and Fred occasionally looked back where the freighters were slouching along.

The sun was low by the time they reached that sump spring amid the cottonwoods again and got down to make camp. Normally, day's end in camp meant relaxation and conversation, but it was difficult when there were corpses lying nearby and two demoralized, filthy, and mute captives squatting in the shade, batting at flies, uninterested in what was going on around them.

Carl came back where Skye and Frank were caring for their horses and said, "Ma'am, are we going to take them freighters to the ranch?"

She arose rubbing dust off her palms. She knew Carl as well as she had known Rand Belton. "We can't hang them, Carl."

He reddened, waited as though pondering a reply to that, then said, "I expect your pa would've, ma'am. Most other folks would. They got it coming."

She considered the short man. "I'm not sure of that, but even so . . . In the morning we'll feed them, saddle their horses, and turn them loose."

Carl had seen something like this coming, so he said, "All right, ma'am. I got a suggestion. Tie the dead ones on their horses and let those other two have them; let them take them along too. It's not up to us to bury 'em anyway."

For Skye it was an easy compromise because she had pondered that problem during the day, and it had gone against her grain to bury any more like those two in the ranch cemetery. The cook and wrangler would have buried the three dead outlaws by now. That was enough.

As Carl went back where Mack and Fred were hunkering at the flickering cooking fire, he squatted and told them what they were to do with Hanford and Ellis. If he expected surprise or disapproval or indignation, he was disappointed.

Neither Fred nor Mack were men of strong opinions or harsh convictions like Carl was. Mack simply said, "I'll be glad to see the last of them corpses. It's bad luck to haul 'em around with you."

Fred was gingerly massaging his bump with grease and said nothing until he was finished, and even then he was not as adamant as he might have been. "Good riddance."

Sam came to the fire, sank down in the grass, and looked at his companions. "You got any of that salve left, Fred?"

It required only a moment for Fred to pass over the dented little tin. All three men watched Sam rub salve into his sore and swollen hands. Carl's mood lightened a little. "I'd have given a month's wages to have seen you whittle that son of a bitch down to size, Sam."

The younger man was passing back the tin when he replied. "Wouldn't have been worth it, Carl. . . . I know something about those bullying big bastards. They got weight and they got size, and specially if it's a hot day, they sweat quick and run out of power fast." He paused, looking at them individually, then changed the subject. "What was wrong with Rand?"

"He quit," Carl said, leaning to feed a twig into the fire.

"I know that. Why?"

Carl concentrated on watching his twig catch fire. "Well, I don't exactly know. I'm not as smart as Rand was. I guess that was why he was a range boss and I never was. He seen things."

Sam shifted his attention to Mack and Fred, but they were sitting as impassive as Indians, also regarding the little supper fire; and when the silence had drawn out long enough, Mack arose to fetch back one of those big army saddlebags with food in it.

Sam accepted the clumsy silence not as an admonition so much but as a wish among the older men to leave this subject. He was willing. His hands were sore for one thing, and he was bone-tired for another. It had been a very long, exhausting day even for someone no older than Sam was. There were many things to remember and think about. He arose, took one of the collapsible canvas buckets, and went over to the spring to fill it.

Hanford and Ellis watched him do this

from nearby shade. Ellis said, "Want some help?" but made no move to arise from the grass.

Sam filled the bucket and looked at them. "Mister," he said quietly, "you're the last man on earth I'd accept help from," and stood up balancing the bucket in one sore hand. "I wouldn't spit on either of you if your guts were on fire."

He was turning away when Ellis had one more question. "What are they going to do with us?"

Hanford, who had not raised his gaze from the ground, looked up now. Sam answered shortly, "You're not hobbled; go ask the boss." Then he returned to the fire.

Mack was doing the cooking. It did not require a lot of skill. There were two pots, one for coffee and one for beans, and a frypan for the meat. Mack had some dry sage which he rolled between his palms under the gaze of Carl and Fred, whose expressions reflected misgivings when he dropped the sage on top of the sizzling meat. He also salted it, which was natural enough. Carl eyed the cooking meat for a while and then said, "Sagebrush is for goats, Mack."

There was no reply to that until the aroma of cooking food reached them all, then Mack smiled across the fire at the short man. "Then I expect you wouldn't like this, Carl. . . . There's some four-day-old biscuits in the saddlebag."

Carl arose and stalked out to look at the horses.

CHAPTER 21

Settling Up

Even though they struck camp early and made only two rest halts to favor the animals, they did not have the Cameron ranch rooftops in sight until midafternoon.

The riding had been easier without Hanford, Ellis, or the two dead men, and whether Carl had approved or not, his bleakness gradually faded as the day advanced; and once, when he and Frank were riding stirrup he leaned on the horn and said, "Some hot water to shave in, a dousing at the creek and some clean clothes, and I'll feel human again. . . . I guess a man could call it a good ending, couldn't he?"

Frank nodded. "Yeah. One headache and two sore fists as opposed to two men killed, another beaten all to hell, and the last one scairt out of his wits."

Carl meticulously drew a very small cube of fuzz-encrusted Kentucky twist from a shirt pocket and while using a thumbnail to get rid of most of the lint before plugging half the tobacco into his mouth, he said, "By my calculations we're still short one man." He tongued the cud into position and looked at Frank. "That's assumin' the wrangler got back, and also assumin' the horseshoer came back with him. Which I doubt. We'd be short two hands then, wouldn't we?"

Frank turned slowly to gaze at the short man. Perhaps Carl was not fishing for information, and then again maybe he was. In either case Frank had little to say. "It will take a little sorting out, for a fact, but not until we've all had a decent meal, a lot of sleep, and like you said, a chance to clean up."

If Carl had indeed been prying, he had to be settled with that answer. He stood in his stirrups, watching the yard come fully into view. It was home and Carl had a strong homing instinct.

Skye came up front and pointed. "I saw five men up there, Frank."

No one else had. In fact none of the others had seen anyone at all up in the yard, but they were still a fair distance out when Skye made that announcement. But from this point on everyone watched, more curious than bothered by the possibility that she had been correct.

She was indeed correct. While they were still a mile out a man strolled up out of the barn and leaned on the rack watching them approach. He called, and other men appeared.

Carl was staring from narrowed eyes when he spoke. "I make out Homer and Jim. None of them other fellers is the horseshoer."

Skye entered the yard in the lead, with the sun against her face even with her hat brim pulled low. The men at the rack straightened up, silent and waiting. Jim was there, still wearing his arm shoved into the front of his shirt, and the *cocinero* was also there, sweaty and handicapped by his weight and years-long lack of physical activity, but the other three men were strangers.

When Skye reined back the three strangers nodded in her direction, showing reserve, but Homer went over to take her reins smiling like a big puppy.

The riders dismounted. Instead of leading their animals inside to the saddle pole, they stood out there, waiting.

One of the strangers was a man with oily dark skin and the kind of black hair that usually went with dark eyes. But his eyes were an almost ash-blue color. He was sinewy and graying, with a granite jaw and a wide, almost lipless mouth. But he had a good smile and as he addressed Skye Cameron, he demonstrated a degree of gallantry not uncommon among range men. He inclined his head once, then smiled and said, "I'm Deputy U.S. Marshal Walter Whiting. These gents are Les Cullen an' Dave Manning. Deputy sheriffs from Carterville — if you know where that is, ma'am. A town about three hunnert miles east of here." Having got all that said, the U.S. marshal continued to smile. "You'll be Miss Cameron?"

Skye nodded as Homer led her horse into the barn to be cared for. "Yes, I'm Skye Cameron, Marshal. Is there something I can do for you?"

The chalky-eyed man's smile faded out a little. "We rode in day before yestiddy. Accordin' to the cook, couple hours after you left . . . I thought we'd ought to stay until you got back so's you'd know what else we did. We helped the cook and your wrangler bury Charley Burris, Eli Madden, an' Lem Tucker. It helps, ma'am, to make a positive identification."

Frank turned to lead his horse into the

barn. The other men followed his example. Skye pulled off her gloves as she watched the riders walk away. Th pale-eyed federal officer was studying her. Eventually he said, "Another reason we stayed was beause we'd like to hear what happened when those three men got killed."

Skye's gaze returned to the lawman. "Who were they, Marshal; what had they done?"

"Dynamited a stage company safe over in Carterville, shot an old man who was night watchman, and a few miles north of town on their way out of the country, stopped a coach, robbed it, and killed a passenger who didn't want to give up his watch and finger ring. They also took the mail pouches. It would have been a federal offense even if they hadn't taken the mail because the money they got from the safe was a government payroll. They went into the mountains and finally turned west. I'm a fair tracker, ma'am, but if they hadn't taken three fresh horses from a stump rancher about sixty miles east of here, maybe we wouldn't have been able to keep on their trail." The sinewy man paused, smiled, and said, "I expect you could say they was successful at robbery and failures as horse thieves."

Frank, Sam, and the other riders sauntered

out of the barn and stood in fading hot sunlight, listening and watching the federal lawman. Skye looked in their direction as she spoke. "Marshal, Mister Cutler and Mister Morton and I went after them. When the fight started I was back in the timber. Mister Cutler can give you the details." She had not smiled up until now. "They haven't eaten lately. Maybe you could go with them over to the cookhouse and talk." She smiled and turned in the direction of the main house.

Marshal Whiting watched her for a moment or two, then turned. "Mister Cutler?"

Frank nodded.

The lawman smiled again. "Maybe the three of us could do like the boss lady said."

Sam moved ahead to follow the lawman in the direction of the cookhouse. Behind them, Fred made a friendly gesture to the pair of deputy sheriffs. "It's hot out here. If you gents'd care to use the bunkhouse while we get cleaned up, you'd be right welcome. . . . After supper we usually get up a little game of stud."

Homer hastened across the yard. Normally at this time of day he would have had supper ready for the crew. Today, he'd had no warning that they might arrive and had nothing prepared. He pushed inside wheezing hard and while Sam, Frank, and Marshal Whiting drew off cups of tepid coffee, Homer got as busy as a cat in a box of shavings.

Frank dropped his hat on the table, conscious of how he looked, because he did not feel much better. Sam's bruised, swollen hands held Marshal Whiting's gaze for a moment until he raised his eyes as Frank began speaking.

What had happened in that high meadow had happened only one way, and was therefore subject to a retelling in only one way. Frank started with the loss of his horse and stopped talking ten minutes later. The only sound during his recitation was Homer amid his pans over at the wood stove.

Marshal Whiting considered the backs of his hands during the quiet which followed Frank's silence. Eventually he said, "What did you fetch back with you?" and slowly raised his chalky eyes.

Frank understood exactly what was in the lawman's mind. "One pouch with some mail in it, and as much as I could stuff into the sack that was lying around. They'd been using letters to start their fires. . . . And three packets of greenbacks. They're over at the bunkhouse."

"Did you count the money, Mister Cutler?"

252

Frank hadn't. In fact he had paid only in-difference to the three small packets tied with fishline. "Nope. Sam found it in their saddle-bags, Marshal. We put it back in there and that's all. How much did they steal?"

"Nine thousand dollars."

Frank and Sam stared.

Whiting's smile returned. "A lot of money, eh?"

That was an understatement. Frank Cutler had never earned more than thirty dollars a month in his life and had never seen more than five hundred dollars at one time. Sam had never even seen that much in one sum. He wagged his head. "Sure didn't seem like that much to me, Marshal."

The pale eyes moved to Sam. They did not move for a while, then Whiting made a little shrug of the shoulders. "We'll go count it di-rectly. One other thing, gents. The stage com-pany put out a one thousand dollar reward. Altogether, there was four thousand on the heads of Tucker, Madden, and Burris. That's from the authorities in three states and two territories." Whiting turned to watch Homer head for the doorway, and turned back only after the cook began beating on his mealtime iron on the porch. "Even if I'd caught up to them, I can't accept rewards. That's federal law." He reached for his half-empty cup and drained it, then arose. "It'll take time. Those things always do, but I'll make out my report, and someday when all the facts get put together, you fellers will start getting the rewards." He stepped back from the table. "Let's go count the money and look at the mail pouch."

As they were leaving, Mack, Fred, Carl, and the breed horseman with his arm inside his shirt hurried past. Homer stood out of the way, then also went back inside.

There were shadows in the yard, it was still warm, and from a great distance came the bawling of a mammy cow who could not find her calf, and if the calf had a bellyful of milk he would not respond so the bawling would continue.

At the bunkhouse Marshal Whiting examined the pouch, sifted briefly through the letters, then turned as Sam dropped those three packets of money on the table. While Frank and Sam watched, the lawman flicked the corners of crisp greenbacks, paused once to look back at them, then went on counting until he was finished and tossed down the last packet. "Shy four hundred," he announced. "It's darned seldom all recovered anyway. Sometimes they cache it, other times they mail it back home to a wife or someone, and most often they spend it. This time I don't think they spent it. They weren't near any towns or settlements once they turned west. . . . Well hell, that's someone else's worry." He smiled. "What would you fellers do with four thousand dollars?"

Frank had no ready answer to that. He'd never had to think about it before and could not possibly have given a prompt answer now. He turned toward Sam, and the younger man grinned. "Buy a new set of blankets for my bedroll, and maybe a new pair of boots."

Whiting laughed and Frank grinned.

They returned to the cookhouse for supper. Afterward, with the poker session getting under way at the bunkhouse, Frank and Sam went down to the creek to bathe. From the settling darkness Sam called down where Frank was soaping. "I been thinking. It could make a man worry, Frank. I got no idea what to do with a lot of money because I never figured I'd have a lot." Sam stepped into the creek and gasped.

"In that case," Frank called back, "don't do anything with it. It don't get stale like biscuits and it won't rot if you keep it dry. It'll just lie there and be handy for the day you need it. And we don't have it yet. Maybe we won't have it for a hell of a long time."

"Frank?"

"Yeah."

"Cameron's a good outfit."

"Yes it is."

"Are you going to stay?"

Frank got out of the water. He was much warmer out of it than in it. "For a while anyway," he called back. "You?"

"For a while anyway. I guess every range rider's got to work at least once for a lady boss. . . . She's pretty savvy."

Frank smiled as he dressed. "She offered me Belton's job on the ride back this morning."

"The hell. You goin' to take it?"

"I guess I'll make a try at it, Sam. I've been a top hand but never a range boss."

"I'll help."

Frank considered his hat by the puny starlight, eased it on his head, and sat down to pull on his boots. "Sure you'll help," he called out. "Partners help each other."

"My pa used to say that for real friends, when one's got a biscuit, the other one's got half."

"Sam, your pa was pretty savvy."

For a while as Sam made noise up in his willow thicket, there was nothing more said, but after he was dressed and joined Frank to walk back toward the lights, he looked at the main house and made a too-casual comment. "Mack and Fred got a notion the reason Rand left was because of you."

"Did they tell you that?"

"No, I was out back when they were talkin' in the barn. Mack said Rand's always been soft on her, but somehow it never worked out between them. . . . He said the reason Rand decided to quit was because when we came back from that high meadow fight, you and her was something besides the boss and a hired man. Fred said he saw that too."

Frank breathed deeply of pure night air. There were lights still burning over at the cookhouse. "Fred and Mack," he told the younger man, "are a pair of old grannies. . . . I think I'll go see if Homer wants to cut my hair tonight."

They parted out behind the bunkhouse.

Homer was sitting alone at the long cook-shack table, drinking black coffee which was about one-third malt whiskey. When Frank entered he said, "Still hungry?"

"No. Full as a tick. I need a shearing, Homer."

The cook leaned back. "You got two bits?"

Frank put the silver coin on the table. "If

you'd rather we can wait until tomorrow."

"Naw. You're dang near steppin' on it now. That first day you rode into the yard with the old bronco I thought you looked more like a sheepherder than a range man. . . . Fetch that lamp. We got to do this outside on the porch; otherwise hair might get into the food. . . . I got a horseshoe keg out there. . . . I'll get my shears and comb. . . . Damned scissors aren't very sharp."

They weren't sharp at all. In fact they worried off more hair than they cut, and they pulled, but Homer had Frank Cutler where he wanted him. He ignored it when Frank winced and insisted on having the details of everything that had happened since he and the others had left the yard with Hanford and his alleged possemen.

When he was finished extracting information and cutting hair, he got a cracked hand mirror. Frank was surprised. He had not expected to look as good as he did. Homer was evidently a man of many talents. He had in fact done as good a job under adverse conditions as many barbers had done for Frank Cutler under ideal conditions.

Frank arose scratching the back of his neck. He dug out an additional quarter dollar and shoved it into the cook's hand. Homer was so pleased that he invited Frank inside where they could sit in undisturbed conversation while drinking spiked coffee.

CHAPTER 22

Crows and Cake

After Marshal Whiting and his companions had eaten and saddled up, there was a brief exchange of humorous comments about the stud poker session the night before, then they waved and left the yard.

Skye had not appeared last night after she had left everyone down in front of the barn, and she did not appear in the morning until after the lawmen had departed. The men were out back catching horses when she entered the barn; she found Mack in there and sent him to ask Frank to meet her out front.

After Mack had delivered his message, and Frank walked away, Fred winked at Mack. Neither Carl nor the one-armed breed noticed.

The sun was teetering upon the farthest curve of the world, easterly, and it was cold even though according to the almanacs summer had finally arrived. But at this elevation there were no really warm dawns the way there were far southward.

Frank's coat was not buttoned, but Skye's coat was. There were split-hide roping gloves showing from her coat pockets, too, and she was dressed for the saddle. Frank went over to the rack and said "Good morning."

She did not smile. "Good morning, Frank. The work starts today and we've lost a lot of time. . . . I still need a range boss."

His eyes showed something close to humor. When she was like this she was not just blunt, her voice was crisp and businesslike. It tickled him. "I'll be glad to try, ma'am, if you're willing to — "

"I asked you not to call me ma'am. . . . I'm perfectly willing to see you do the job." The green eyes never left his face. "Someone has to show you the areas where Cameron cattle usually graze . . . the salt logs and water holes and such like." Suddenly she looked down and got very busy pulling on the gloves. "First off I'd better tell the others you are replacing Rand. Then Carl can straw-boss today — start the gather with the men because he's familiar with the range." The gloves were on and the green eyes came up. "Starting tomor-

row, they will take their orders from you."
She waited, knowing he would have something to say.

"And I take my orders from you, Skye?"

"Yes." She continued to watch his face. "Frank, since my pa died I've run into this thing about range men disliking taking orders from a woman. Most of them don't even like the idea of taking their wages from a woman. . . . That's all right with me. I can't change the prejudice. Maybe someday it will change, but until then, I know it would have made things a lot easier if I'd been born a man. But I wasn't, and what it boils down to is this: I own Cameron ranch. I also run it. I grew up on this place, know its boundaries and the work from back to front, and have had more experience cowboying our land than anyone except my father, who made me learn it all. I have followed a policy of compromise. I know what should be done, and when it should be done. I also know that men like Carl Hopper would quit the first week I ramrodded the work. That's why I never bossed the men very much, but I did boss Rand. Then, it was up to him to boss the riders."

Frank listened to all this with poker-faced interest. When she had finished speaking, he said, "You've got experienced men, Skye, and they're loyal. That kind doesn't usually need bossing. I know because I've been a man like that for a long time. They take to showing a lot better than they take to bossing. . . . Still want me to try it?"

She relaxed a little. "Yes . . . Would you do something for me?"

"Sure."

"I left my spurs on the porch . . . "

He nodded and started walking. Once, he looked back. She was no longer in sight. She had not forgot the damned spurs; she had not wanted him in the barn when she told the riders he was to be the new range boss.

Well, hell, he already knew women did not think the way men did. It had never bothered him. It did not bother him now as he found the spurs and took them down to the barn to her. But for a fact, if he was going to do the ramrodding for her, he was going to have to learn a lot more about the way women thought than he knew now.

Carl took the other riders out the back of the barn where they mounted and jogged almost due westward. Frank did not finish saddling until the riders were half a mile out, riding bunched and probably in earnest discussion of what was probably not exactly a surprise to them.

Homer, draping soggy flour-sack dish towels from an old rope stretched between porch uprights over at the cookhouse, watched his employer and Frank Cutler leave the yard together heading northward. He made a little clucking sound. Up until he saw this, he'd had no idea. . . . The men rarely confided in him. Mack *had* told him Rand had quit, but that was all.

Homer's world had been getting smaller for many years. He had not been able to ride out for a long time. Now, his interest was confined to the ranch yard, to whatever scraps of discussion he heard, usually at the supper table, to the hints of gossip he gleaned, and to the people he lived in isolation with at the Cameron ranch.

He would have enjoyed being able to ride out again, but since that was no longer possible he did not really dislike the pattern his existence had taken over the past years. And because he was as he was, Homer had often speculated about Skye, who was in his eyes a beautiful woman. He had always been partial to stocky ones with strong backs; for a fact they bore up a lot better than those tall, scrawny ones they were always putting on the fronts of magazines, and who weren't built for anything but maybe reaching a flour sack off a tall cupboard, or maybe running — and who the hell needed a woman who could run, that was why the Good Lord had given horses four legs instead of two, so they could do the running.

He finished with the dish towels and went back inside to plunge an arm deep into the flour barrel and bring his hand back out with a whiskey bottle in it. He made the mixture a little stronger this time: half java and half malt whiskey.

A flight of crows passed northward in one of their shabby formations, caterwauling in their raucous way. They were not exactly harbingers of summer because they had never really left the high prairie country, but they were more in evidence after good weather arrived. Homer sipped his coffee ignoring the crows and renewing his speculations about Skye getting settled into double harness. For a damned fact any ranch, and that included the Cameron outfit, needed someone ramrodding it who wore heavy cowhide work gloves, not the damned split-hide, measly soft deerskin gloves women wore.

The crows were almost out of earshot now, their garrulousness little more than an echo in the yard. But two miles out, riding at an easy lope, when they passed Frank and Skye,

265

Frank glanced upwards. In his experience crows had always seemed to be an epitome of raffishness. They were always to be found where there were people. Their attitude was one of opportunistic dishonesty. They made their living from the mistakes of earthbound creatures and were definitely derisive about it. He watched them until Skye said, "Next to buzzards, I dislike crows most."

He laughed. He did not dislike crows. He did not particularly like them, but there were very few things Frank Cutler actually disliked.

Two more miles northward Skye veered eastward toward a hollowed cedar log which had no grass growing within fifteen feet of it in any direction. Cameron riders made casual sashays out this way occasionally, and when the log was empty they loaded sacks of rock salt into a wagon and came out to refill it.

Altogether, there were eleven of those salt logs on the ranch, and each had been strategically placed so that the riders could find cattle almost any time they rode near one. It made rounding up, as well as keeping an eye on the livestock, a lot easier than it would have been if there had been no salt logs.

They halted briefly. The log still had a few granules of salt in it. Frank said, "Enough for another couple of weeks," and Skye nodded as she reined away.

"The cattle aren't over here anyway. They'll be out west toward the broken country. We push them to summer feed in March."

"Where I come from that's a mite late."

"It's colder in this country, Frank. The days are warm but as long as the nights freeze, grass doesn't come up good." She watched as he shed his coat and tied it behind the saddle. A short distance onward she did the same with her coat. She was wearing a white shirt. He had never seen her ride out before in anything but a blue work shirt.

They continued eastward for another hour, then she led the way up atop a round knoll and halted to point. "See that little pocket of fir trees?"

He saw them. They looked about the size of toothpicks in the clear morning air. "Yes . . . Your line is over there?"

"Approximately. Perhaps five miles farther east. We graze this country off first." She turned to ride back down to the flat country again, and now they loped westward, with the foothills about four miles northward. He eyed the foothills, and the darkly forested uplands behind them. They were a long distance east of where they had entered those mountains on that manhunt that had ended in the death of three outlaws, but it was the same string of mountains.

She brought his attention around with a question. "What were you thinking?"

He met her gaze. "You know what I was thinking."

She did not press it. When they slackened off a little with the heat increasing, she aimed for an arroyo with treetops showing above its edges and sashayed until she found what she had been seeking, a wide trail leading down into the arroyo where there was underbrush, smashed grass, and pines. The area still smelled of cattle even though none had been down here in a long while.

She went unerringly to a flowing spring, swung off, and removed the horse's bridle after hobbling it, and with her back to Frank, unlashed the saddlebags, flung them over her shoulder, and went over to the shaded little spring with its surrounding area of dark grass.

Frank was in no hurry to finish caring for his horse. He was beginning to recognize some of her characteristics, one of which was that when she kept her back to him, she was either annoyed or self-conscious. She had no reason to be annoyed with him, so it had to be the other thing.

When he went over and dropped down to drink, and, facing her, pitched his hat aside, she had food spread on top of a red-checkered tablecloth. It had not come from the cookhouse; the only covering used on the table there was a worn and marred wide strip of floor covering so shiny from use it was slippery.

She waited until he was ready and then said, "Homer had nothing to do with this," and raised her eyes in a quick, quizzical look.

He smiled. "I didn't think he had. . . . I didn't know you could cook."

She rocked back, reddening slightly. "I can cook very well."

He wanted to laugh. Instead he began to eat, and when he noticed how she shot glances at him from the corner of her eye, he made an exaggerated effort to chew slowly and frown a little, as though he knew how things should taste, which in fact he did not know, unless they were terrible or rancid.

"Very good," he told her, finally. "For a fact, you can cook."

She dropped her head as she ate. "I don't do it often. . . . Since pa died I haven't had to . . . haven't felt like doing it."

He understood that. He too had lived alone for long periods, and preparing a meal had

had no appeal to him either under those circumstances. He refilled the tin plate and poured more coffee for them both.

"Frank?"

"Yes."

"I forgot to mention something when I offered you the foreman's job . . . I'd want you to stay on, not maybe quit in a year or so." She was not looking at him. She pointed. "That's chocolate cake under the napkin." She still did not look at him.

He peeked beneath the napkin. Unless a man was in a town, chocolate cakes were only for Christmas, very special occasions. He said, "I wouldn't take the job if I didn't expect to do it right and to stay on. There's something I never told you, too; except for straw-bossing now and then I've never been much more than a top hand."

"That's all right. What you don't know I can show you . . . I mean, about the boundaries, the different parts of the range, things like that. And how we shorten up in autumn so the cattle will be closer in case of blizzards."

She held out her empty plate for him to cut the cake. He did a good job of it and then resumed eating until his own plate was cleaned and he could also have a piece of cake.

Again, he went through that exaggerated routine of savoring the cake, and this time as she watched, her stare was not as unsure as it had been before. She said, "I hope you choke."

He laughed, and she smiled back at him. "It's one of the best chocolate cakes I ever ate, Skye. Most likely it is *the* best one. You got abilities a man would never suspect from looking at you."

Her smile whisked out. She reddened. After a long moment of struggling, she said, "You want to know something, Frank? You can be the most aggravating human I've ever known."

He went on eating cake, completely unruffled. When it was safe to speak he said, "I shouldn't do that, should I?"

"Do what, fill your mouth too full?"

"No. Tease you. I apologize. I knew you'd get red in the face when I said that."

For a while she watched him, then she held out her plate again, and while he was putting another wedge of cake on it, she said, "I . . . don't mind being teased. But no one has done it since my father died. He was the biggest tease who ever lived, and I loved him very much."

Her lips remained parted after saying that,

her eyes darkened in chagrin, and she ducked her head to begin on the second piece of cake. This time he saw the color flood into her face.

CHAPTER 23

Normal Times

Carl had found trouble on the west range. A band of cattle had been grazing off a sunken place of smelly marshland because it had tall grass, and now he'd found the beginnings of hoofrot.

It was not widespread, but enough animals were suffering from it to make Carl worry. He told Frank about it over supper, and a strategy was worked out. Frank and Carl would team up. Mack and Fred would do the same. Sam and the wrangler would work on the ground, and that night Frank would make the disinfectant mix Sam and the wrangler would apply to the infected hooves.

Any way a hired rider looked at something like this, it was not simply hard work, it was also dangerous. Range cattle were very different from milk cows.

Later, when Frank and Sam were in the barn making their pastelike medicine, which had a terrible smell, Skye walked in, wrinkled her nose, and came down and watched. Frank explained why they were making the medicine. She considered the tub full and said, "What's in it?"

"Powdered blue vitriol, sulfur, air-slacked lime, and some of that pine tar we found in the harness room."

"It's too thick, Frank. My father used to make a mixture that was darker and more watery. It was easier to put on with a paintbrush or a rag swab."

He straightened up drying his hands and looking at her. Sam was grunting as he worked a pitchfork handle through the medicine and ignored them both.

Frank took her arm and led her out front where a sickle moon shone amid a rash of golden-colored stars. He put aside the rag and leaned on the tie rack gazing at the ground. After a while he said, "Skye . . . "

She held up a hand. "I know. I knew it the minute you straightened up and reached for that rag. Well, I was just telling you how pa used to do it."

He let her finish. He also allowed a moment of silence to settle between them before speaking again. "But he's not here, Skye, and I've used this mixture with a lot of success for something like twenty years. . . . Now then, if you want to use his mixture, why then —"

"No. Maybe if it's thicker it will stay on longer. . . . I could ride out there and maybe help tomorrow."

She was lovely by moonlight, and she looked more nearly eighteen than whatever she was — he had guessed her to be maybe twenty-five, when in fact she was thirty-three.

He had matured in the old mold; women-folk were never allowed around a working corral or at a doctoring ground. It was bad enough to get cow-kicked or trampled or get your air knocked out, but the injury was invariably compounded by a man not being able to express himself at the top of his lungs to ease the pain.

He asked a question. "Did your pa want you around the corrals or marking grounds when they were working?"

He hadn't. "My pa was old-fashioned, Frank. I've heard all the words."

"It's your outfit, Skye."

"But you don't want me out there."

"Well, no, that's not it. I'd like very much to have you where I am — but not when there's going to be a lot of bad talk."

She smiled at him. "I still think it's too thick," she said, and walked briskly in the direction of the main house.

Sam had the mixture a uniform, sickly color when Frank returned and hunted in the harness room until he found a jug of coal oil. He took that out, poured it in, and at Sam's questioning look he explained. "Might be a tad too thick . . . Now then, let's stir it some more, then put it into the buckets."

Sam leaned on the pitchfork gazing across the large tub. "Then why in the hell didn't we put the coal oil in before I mixed it? It would have been a lot easier to work."

Frank did not respond, but when they had the buckets ready to be loaded into a wagon in the morning, and they had gone out back to scrub, he said, "It'll be easier to put on."

Sam raised up shaking off water. "Know what I think? *She* told you it needed thinning." Sam turned and started walking. "Homer's going to cut my hair tonight. See you later."

When Frank entered the bunkhouse all the conversation stopped, then it started up again on a fresh topic. He acted as though he had no idea that they had probably been discussing him, and most likely in relation to their employer.

Carl wrinkled his nose. "That medicine ought to work; my ma used to say medicine ain't worth a darn unless it smells rotten and tastes even worse."

They did not have the poker session going that night. They had been speculating and gossiping a little instead, so when Sam returned they were all getting ready to bed down. Sam did not join them, he grabbed his towel and went stamping out the back way in the direction of the creek. All he said was, "Homer lets more hair go down a man's back than he lets fell on the porch."

Frank lay back waiting for someone to blow down the lamp mantel. When the room was finally plunged into darkness he folded both arms under the back of his head, looking straight up. He was still like that, but sound asleep, when Sam came back to finally bed down also.

By the time dawn arrived they had all been fed and were either rigging out their horses or harnessing the work team to the old wagon.

As Frank finally swung into the saddle he saw a light at the main house. There was no reason that he knew of for Skye to be rolling out this early. As he reined around in the wake of the wagon, a thought occurred to him. She was going to ride out where they would be working the cattle today. Darn fool women anyway.

Carl and the breed, bundled inside coats and with their hats pulled low, rode ahead in an easy lope. The wagon was slow, with Fred on the seat smoking his first cigarette of the day. When Frank came up, Fred said, "You ever been to Arizona? I never have, but I've heard it said it's never this cold down there, not even in winter."

Frank had been in Arizona. "The northern part gets just as cold before sunrise, and the southern part doesn't, but it gets so hot during the daytime in summer, you can fry eggs on the rocks, and unless you know where there's water, you can die of thirst without any effort at all."

Fred was a stubborn man at times. "Well, damn it, there's got to be some place where a man don't freeze his *chingalee* off every blessed morning."

"There is," Frank replied. "Heaven. They tell me it's always warm and real pleasant up there."

Fred spat out his smoke and straightened forward again as he said, "No. I ain't ready for that yet."

It was a long trip because even though the riders finally loped ahead to make a gather of sore-footed animals, they could not begin the doctoring until the much slower wagon came up.

Then they had to eat, so by the time the roping started, it was one o'clock with enough heat to make a man sweat when he was standing still.

It was bruising work, the air turned blue, there was thick dust, and when a man went to the wagon for a drink of water, swarms of flies swooped down in search of salty sweat, which seemed to be a particular elixir to them.

Skye did not arrive. Frank occasionally wasted a moment or two scanning the back trail expecting to see her. He never did, and by the time they had worked through nearly all the sore-footed cattle, he decided she was not coming, and that made him simultaneously pleased and disappointed. The last time he went for water and met Sam over there, he said, "You'd figure an owner would come out here and see how bad this hoofrot is."

Sam leaned and looked upward wearing an expression of baffled irritation. "Frank, I heard you tell her out front of the barn last night you didn't want her out here."

Frank replaced the sacking-wrapped water bottle and turned, pulling on his gloves as he watched the other men snaking in another fighting, bawling, slobber-flinging, wild-eyed cow. As though Sam had not spoken he said, "Let's get back to it, Sam. It'll be sundown directly."

They had not been racing the sun, but if they had been, it would have been a draw. When they led the tired horses back to the wagon for a bait of grain, and someone started passing the last of the water bottles around, the sun sank slowly and unnoticed beyond the westernmost mountains.

The men were battered, bruised, tired to the marrow, and disinclined to talk very much. Carl made the only statement. "If I was ramrodding this outfit, I'd send off for one of them ripping plows they use back east, and run me a danged ditch for two miles to the lower ground, so's most of this stinking water would drain away from here."

They loaded the wagon, pulled tired and bruised bodies over leather, and started home with rusty sunlight behind them and much nearer a lot of sore-footed cows kicking and pawing because the medicine they had been dosed with caused more immediate discomfort than the hoofrot which afflicted them.

A couple of miles along Frank turned to Carl and said, "We'll go back in the morning and push the cattle to dry ground."

Carl nodded agreement, and Sam, who had been silent since starting back, rode up beside Frank with an idea he had been perfecting as he rode along.

"Suppose we used that branding chute in the main corral, that narrow one that squeezes a cow so she can't go any way but forward. . . . We could put planks at the bottom, then pour that hoofrot medicine in there thick as molasses and just drive them through in a long line. It'd sure be a lot easier on them, and us, than what we did today. An' we could drive 'em through several times, instead of dosing 'em just once."

Frank was rolling a smoke as he listened. Afterward, when he was lighting up, he eyed the younger man. The more Frank thought about it, the more reasonable it seemed to be. He said, "We'll talk about it, Sam," and raised his head at the movement dead ahead through the settling dusk.

It was Skye driving the top buggy. They met her while the dusk was turning increasingly dark, and she turned to drive back with them. She asked if they had dosed all the sore-footed cattle. He told her that they had, and when she looked the men over and said dryly they looked as though they had been through

281

a battle, he told her of Sam's idea. She drove a considerable distance in silence, as though considering the suggestion.

When they reached the yard, Homer's cookhouse lamps were glowing, and someone brought a lantern to the barn while they cared for the animals; then they trooped out back to wash.

Skye cared for the driving horse by herself, and even picked up both shafts and backed the buggy into its shed without assistance.

She left them, as she ordinarily did, when they were ready to head over for supper. Frank stood briefly on the cookhouse porch watching her go to the main house. He'd had a feeling that she had wanted to say more than she'd said on the ride back. Well, there would be another day. Right now he was as hungry as were the other men, but more than that, he was sore and tired.

They all acted as though they had been somewhat revived by Homer's heavy meal, but when they reached the bunkhouse not even Fred, who was the most enthusiastic stud player on the ranch, mentioned starting up a session.

It was too late to head for the creek, so they retired without bathing and slept like dead men until habit awakened them shortly before dawn, and what they had not noticed last night, or in the evening, was abundantly noticeable in the morning. Even the air smelled different. It was going to rain.

After breakfast Frank lined out the usual chores when ranch hands were yardbound. Mack and Fred strung out harnesses on the saddle pole and made repairs when they were needed, and otherwise soaped and lightly oiled all the leather.

The rain arrived promptly. It was warm and steady and welcome any summertime. Frank and Sam forged blank horseshoes at the shoeing shed, another chore which was ordinarily done when the men could not ride out.

Carl came over to the shed after racking up stove wood at the bunkhouse on the rear porch and hauling three buckets of ash from the bunkhouse stove. He squinted upward from just inside the shed's wide front opening, then turned and said, "It'll be a good year. When rains come this early, there'll be plenty of water later to keep the grass coming."

Sam was sizing and racking the plates and said nothing. Frank, sleeves up as he measured and marked the bar steel, only nodded.

Carl eyed them a while, then concentrated on Frank. "The boss wants to see you," he announced as though it were something trivial.

Frank put down the soap and balanced the bar steel atop the anvil. He looked at Carl. "Now?"

"Yeah, now. I met her out back when I was tiering the firewood. She's at the main house."

Sam got an anxious expression on his face. Carl, though, was not only unworried, he held his face blank as though unwilling to have Sam or Frank guess what he was thinking. Then he turned and began another, this time, more elaborate, long study of the gray overcast which seemed almost low enough for a man to reach out and touch.

Frank sluiced off at the bucket, rolled his sleeves down, and reached for his hat. After he was crossing the yard through a light but constant downpour, Carl went over to the anvil, squinted to find Frank's marks on the bar steel, and started to roll up his sleeves. With his back to Sam he said with studied casualness. "If there's one thing we never have enough of around here, it's horseshoes when we need them." Then Carl went to work.

CHAPTER 24

Rain

There was a dry-oak fire in the parlor which gave off heat, blue flame, no noise, and almost no smoke. The room was large and poorly lighted from outside. There were only two windows, each in the front wall so that Skye's father, who had built this house, had immediate access to the only view he cared about — down across the ranch yard to the north range, and much farther toward the far mountains.

Skye was wearing a dress. She looked particularly feminine in it, but perhaps because Frank had never seen her in the role of a total woman before, it made him uncomfortable to see her that way now.

She had done something to her hair, too, and whatever it was, it shocked him when she stepped into the light because she had a hint of silver over the ears. He accepted the mug of coffee she offered and met her green gaze.

She stepped closer to the window, holding her cup. "I love springtime rains, but not if they last more than one day." She turned. "Someone's working in the shoeing shed."

"Sam and Carl. In this kind of weather it's customary to do the chores. They're making plates."

"You never make anything easy for me, do you?"

He eyed her carefully. "I'll never miss a chance to make things easy for you, Skye."

They stood facing one another with the whisper of rainfall overhead. "It was pleasant yesterday up at the spring."

He nodded.

"Frank, that's what I mean. You never make it easy for me."

He leaned and placed the cup on a little table. As he straightened up he looked steadily at her as he said, "Skye, let's start over, and this time you tell me the rules."

She sighed and half turned away. "There are no rules. . . . Would you like some whiskey in your coffee?"

"No thanks." He knew her fairly well by now. He did not understand her mood today, but he knew *his* mood. She had a fragrance of flowers he had not noticed before, and she was dressed as a woman, and she was very handsome. And finally, he'd had troubling thoughts, and feelings, for a long time now. Last night lying in his bunk staring upward into the darkness, he had confronted something that had begun to bother him two weeks earlier. He could not be around her much longer without putting what he felt into words. The moment he did that, their relationship would be forever changed — he would no longer be able to function as her foreman because if he remained at Cameron ranch there would always be tension between them.

It wasn't losing the job; he'd lost jobs before and had always managed to find new ones. He said, "Skye, we've got a problem. . . . Well, *I've* got a problem."

She turned, saying nothing.

He grinned at her. "Now it's you who doesn't help much."

"How can I help, Frank, you haven't said what it is."

"Well . . . it goes sort of like this. I think we could work the ranch, you as owner, me as foreman, without a whole lot of arguments."

"Go on."

"Well . . . it's you."

The green eyes were as steady as stone.

"I . . . You know, light, summer rains like this sure make good grass, don't they?"

"Frank Cutler, I'm going to punch you!"

"Well . . . now don't get mad."

"I don't get mad."

"Yes you do. Real easy, in fact."

"I won't this time. . . . Are we going to stand up through all this?"

He did not even look around for a chair. "It's been growing on me for quite a while, and it's not your fault."

"Frank . . . !"

". . . I'm in love with you, Skye."

She softly said, "I think I'll sit down."

He watched her move to a chair and looked toward the hearth. The fire was almost down to coals. He went over to a large brass bucket, picked out two rounds of dry oak, and placed them carefully in the nest of coals. Activity always made it easier for him to talk, so he stood watching for the rounds to burn, and without turning, he said, "I didn't have to tell you, but it'd be almost impossible not to show it sooner or later. And anyway, a man can't do his job with something like this on his mind all the time."

He turned, finally. She had lighted a lamp on the table beside her chair. Outside, the day was getting increasingly gloomy as it wore along. In lamplight she looked eighteen again, and she was sitting relaxed, watching him, her mouth totally relaxed, her large green eyes unwavering in a grave, almost solemn way.

He went over, retrieved his coffee cup, moved to the window, and set his back to it, looking at her. He almost grinned. "I got quite a problem, haven't I?"

Very slowly her gaze responded to his faint grin. "There are worse problems, Frank. Hoofrot for instance, or blowflies at dehorning time, or . . . other things. . . . Why do you think I'm wearing a dress today . . . ? Can I get you a tad of whiskey for the coffee?"

He looked down into the cup, which was nearly empty. "No thanks I don't need any whiskey, and I don't know why you're wearing a dress today. Maybe because it's raining and you can't go outside."

She drained her own cup and put it aside. "Do you know how old I am?"

He did not know, and although his experience with women was far from extensive, he had good instincts. Right now they told him to avoid a direct answer at all costs, so he said, "I sure don't."

"Thirty-three."

That surprised him. That would make her

eight years older than he had thought she was. "I don't believe it. You look like you are maybe twenty-five."

Her cheeks colored, then she laughed. When that passed she appeared to be struggling with her thoughts, and Frank risked an answer to what he assumed her thoughts might be. "I'm forty-four, and sometimes, like last night when we got back to the yard, I feel eighty-four." He continued to gaze at her. She had a wonderful laugh and a beautiful smile. "Forty-four is old," he said.

She arose, paced to the hearth and turned to face him from over there. "Forty-four in a man is his prime, Frank."

He waited for more but that was all she said. He put aside the cup without draining it and looked at the rack near the door where his hat was hanging.

She spoke instantly. "About your problem . . ."

He did not want to talk about it. "I just had to get it said is all."

"Frank . . . That's what I meant at the spring yesterday when I said you didn't ever make things easy for me. . . . Since we . . . I think from the morning you and Sam rode in with my riders and old Plume more than a month ago . . . You see, you're not helping me now, either."

"Well . . . what am I supposed to say?"

She waited, then smiled at him. "Nothing
. . . When we were up at that big meadow and
I knew someone was going to be killed, I
prayed longer and harder than I've prayed
since I was eight years old. . . . You weren't
even the range boss then, and I was in love
with you."

The soft rainfall fell, there was a prolonged
silence, then Frank broke it by reaching to
pick up his cup and hold it out. "I would like
a tad of whiskey in my coffee now, ma'am."

She made no move to take the cup, but she
moved from the fireplace as she said, "It's in
the kitchen. . . . I'll make us something to
eat. It's about that time, I think."

He followed her out there. It was a large
kitchen, and again, because there was only
one window, much smaller this time, in the
east wall she lighted a lamp. He stood looking
around. She said, "This was the first room my
father built. It was more like a fort. He and
my mother lived in it for seven years before he
could start the rest of the house. She used to
feed the riders at that big old table."

She filled his cup, placed it at the head of
the long old, polished table, placed a bottle
of malt whiskey in front of him, then waited a

moment before turning toward the stove. "Would you like to know something, Frank? I'm as nervous as I've ever been in my life. More nervous than up at the big meadow."

He raised his eyes. "You didn't mean that, Skye; how could you mean anything like that?"

She was turning when he said that. She abruptly turned back. "Why would any woman tell a man something like that if she did not mean it?"

He did not respond.

"Did *you* mean it, Frank?"

"Yes. I wouldn't have said it otherwise."

"That is what I just told you. Neither would I. Neither would any woman." The green eyes were dark. "Would you like to . . . take it back?"

"No. To tell you the truth I feel a lot better now that I've told you. But for you to — "

"Stop doubting, Frank. Stop trying to explain something no one has ever been able to explain before. I don't know how this happens any more than you do. But I meant it, all of it." She pulled down a deep breath. "I am in love with you. I've been in love with you ever since we talked that first time, and you didn't like me. Up at the big meadow I almost. . . ."

He smiled at her. "Skye, I don't have a darned thing but the blue horse and my outfit . . . an' it's not very new."

She let her breath out slowly. "I don't care. . . . And we have that in common, Frank. I don't have anything either — not the things that make a person's life worth living . . . The ranch? You told me I'd die here. I could have told you when you said that that the idea has haunted me for years. Yes, I'll probably die here and be buried out yonder . . . never loved, never married ' . . . the damned spinster boss lady to my last breath. I'll tell you something else, Frank. I had just about made up my mind I would not do it. I'd sell the ranch and go somewhere, and maybe get married. . . . Frank?"

"Yes."

"Well . . . do you want to put some whiskey in that coffee or let it get cold?"

He made no move toward either the cup or the bottle. "Is that what you really started out to say?"

"No. But I'm not supposed to ask that question, you are."

"If you'd marry me, Skye . . . I'd never have to call you ma'am again." He laughed, then pushed back the chair and faced her standing up. "I'd even water down the

293

hoofrot medicine."

Her vision was a little blurry. "You'll never stop teasing, will you?"

"I'll try. Right now I shouldn't, except that I'm as nervous as a cat."

"I'll marry you, Frank."

She came into his arms and pushed her face into his chest, which smelled of forge smoke from the shoeing shed. He raised a hand to tilt her face upward but she resisted. "In a minute," she told him, and sniffled. "Frank, I feel as limp as a rag . . . and scared."

He could feel the solid beat of her heart and the strength of her body full-length. After a while he said, "You don't have to fix something to eat, I'm not hungry."

She raised her face. He kissed her lightly, softly, and for a long time. When he pulled back a little she smiled. "My nose is shiny and my eyes feel puffy . . . and you didn't shave this morning."

"How far is Fort McCall from here?"

"Two days over and two days back in a buggy. A little shorter on horseback . . . except that we can't take as much with us on horseback as we can in a buggy."

"They have a minister?"

"Yes."

"Well . . . there's the work, Skye."

She curved backward in his arms. "There has always been the work, and there always will be the work. It waited before, it can wait again."

He released her. "Well . . . a good early start, if it's stopped raining by morning."

"Whether it's stopped raining or not, Frank," she said, raising a small handkerchief to her face but watching him over the edge of it.

He started to smile, his gaze at her soft and caring and gentle. The rain was still falling but seemed to be diminishing a little, at least it sounded less insistent upon the roof now. It would be clear, come morning. The land would steam and the sun would shine.

THORNDIKE PRESS HOPES you have enjoyed this Large Print book. All our Large Print titles are designed for the easiest reading, and all our books are made to last. Other Thorndike Press Large Print books are available at your library, through selected bookstores, or directly from the publisher. For more information about current and upcoming titles, please call us, toll free, at 1-800-223-6121, or mail your name and address to:

THORNDIKE PRESS
ONE MILE ROAD
P. O. BOX 159
THORNDIKE, MAINE 04986

There is no obligation, of course.